ESPECIALLY FOR GIRLS™ presents

Going on Sixteen

Betty Cavanna

WILLIAM MORROW AND COMPANY
NEW YORK

Edited for Weekly Reader Books and published by
arrangement with William Morrow and Company, Inc.

Library of Congress Cataloging in Publication Data: Cavanna,
Betty, 1909–   Going on sixteen. Summary: Fourteen-year-
old Julie tries to escape her own sense of inadequacy and her
friends' talk of boys and parties by devoting herself to raising
an orphaned collie pup. [1. Self-acceptance—
Fiction.   2. Interpersonal relations—Fiction.
3. Dogs—Fiction]
I. Title. PZ7.C286Go 1985 [Fic] 85-4877
ISBN 0-688-05892-2

Julie stood before the long, cracked mirror in a taffeta evening dress that had been her mother's and nodded at her reflection.

"Thank you, Dick. I'd love to dance."

Did the words sound too stiff?

"Sure, Dick. Love to."

No. That was bad. It made her seem a tomboy.

"I'd like to!"

Said enthusiastically, that was better. Julie raised her left arm to rest it on an imaginary shoulder. She started to hum softly. Then she kicked off her sneakers so that she could stand on tiptoe and pretend she was floating in her partner's arms. Like an actress in the movies.

There was not much room to float in the crowded attic. Boxes and trunks, rickety furniture, and an ancient Singer sewing machine supporting a stack of her mother's canvases hemmed the mirror in on two sides. Dust specks rotated in a shaft of sunlight from the single window, and with every swish of the full skirt a new vast number rose to join them.

Julie admired the full sweep of the skirt over her shoulder, but the sight of her thin back, bare above the low-cut neck of the dress, made her frown. She was thankful that girls today could wear less revealing party dresses, with high backs and sleeves. Then Julie fell to thinking about her own dress—the one she was going to buy tomorrow—the first long dress she had ever planned to own.

It should be a wonderful dress. Julie stopped humming and sank down on her heels as she considered it. She couldn't visualize the color. It might be yellow or it might be pale green, like the new grass on the fields of the farm. But it should be springlike. And very crisp. It should be a dress that would transform her from the everyday Julie

Ferguson into an entirely different girl. This new Julie could never be shy or awkward; she'd go to the Freshman Frolic and have a wonderful time. She'd dance without stumbling. She'd think of bright things to say. She'd be as popular as Anne. Well, maybe not quite *that* popular, but at least she wouldn't be stuck in a corner with a set smile on her face and no invitations to dance.

Julie said aloud, "I hope."

Walking closer to the mirror, she began to study her face critically. Her brown eyes would do. They were set wide apart and the lashes that fringed them were dark and long. Her hair, though, was disturbing. It wasn't brown and it wasn't blond. It was tan, and it was almost straight. Pulled back sternly from her forehead, it gave her an Alice-in-Wonderland look to which her heart-shaped face, winter pale, contributed.

Maybe, thought Julie with an unwelcome thrust of apprehension, Dick won't ask me to dance at all.

There was no reason, really, why he should. Just because they'd gone swimming together, and collected grasshoppers, and built the tree house, these past three summers at the farm. Just because he lived over the hill, rode in on the same school bus, and called her "Peanut." Just because she knew Dick better than any other boy.

But if Dick didn't ask her to dance, who would? Not Hank Martin. He never even looked her way. Not Chunky Spencer. If he were interested in any girl, it was in Anne. Julie reviewed the group of freshman boys who shared her classes and found no one who might rescue her. Her throat began to ache with fear and her image in the mirror lost its novelty and became ridiculous. Even gathering her hair in both hands and twisting it high on her head didn't help. It made her look thinner than ever—"like a picked chicken," Dad would say.

A horn honked outside, and Julie let her hair fall back to her shoulders with a start. If her father wasn't around—if she had to answer the door—she'd have to get out of this rig in a hurry. Fumbling for the hooks, she crossed to the window and looked down.

A polished gray car was parked by the yard gate, and, Julie noticed with relief, Dad was already on his way down from the barn to greet the visitor. Mr. Philip Lonsdale, who was unwinding his lanky but elegant frame from behind the steering wheel, would ordinarily have claimed Julie's undivided attention, but today he had a companion. Leaping from the backseat to land nimbly on the ground was the most beautiful collie Julie had ever seen.

Her fingers paused on the hooks that fastened the dress. Forgetting her haste, Julie knelt on the low windowsill and rubbed a cleaner place on the pane. The dog had rounded the car and was standing against a backdrop of rolling fields brushed with tender grass. Her head was high; her sable-and-white coat was gleaming. Delicately, she sniffed the fresh spring air.

"Scarlet!" Mr. Lonsdale called, and the dog trotted a few paces toward him, turning her head so that she could watch the approach of the man coming down from the barn. Julie forgot her concern over the party. A long sigh of satisfaction swept her, and her eyes remained fastened on the collie.

Scarlet was like a lady in court dress come to visit. She walked the earth of the farm with noble feet, and Julie could imagine her bowing to right and left, accepting admiration. Of course she was a Lonsdale dog. Mr. Lonsdale owned the finest collie kennels in the East, and every now and again he brought one or two of his dogs out to the farm to board. But never a dog like this! Never a collie as magnificent or as queenly.

"Scarlet." Julie whispered the name. Odd, yet right somehow. Later, probably, she would want to touch the dog, stroke the stately head and ruff, but just now to be able to look at her was enough.

A line of poetry she had learned at school flashed through the girl's mind. "Beauty is its own excuse for being." It hadn't meant much when she'd learned it, but now it struck Julie as wonderfully true. Poetry was like that. You memorized it automatically and then later it came back to haunt you.

The collie moved momentarily out of sight behind the car, and Julie's gaze shifted to the two men. Her father, in overalls and boots heavy with wet mud, looked shaggy and unkempt next to his guest. His voice came up to Julie as a deep rumble, but the dog breeder's was higher pitched and she caught an occasional word which told her they were discussing Scarlet. She hoped the collie had come to board for a long time.

Then, as her father shifted position and made a gesture toward the

3

house, an uncomfortable thought swept Julie. Suppose Dad should ask Mr. Lonsdale to come inside! He was apt to. The shabbiness of the farm never seemed to concern him, as it did Julie. He'd be bound to take him straight to the kitchen, because it was the only room on the first floor that was decently warm, this time of year. And down in the kitchen, on a line by the gas stove, was strung—underwear! A slip, panty hose, a bra. Julie's eyes narrowed in alarm and she scrambled off the windowsill and raced down the two flights of narrow stairs.

She was just in time! Her hand swept the line clear as Mr. Lonsdale and her father entered the door. Trapped, she turned with one arm behind her. Then, too late, she remembered the dress.

Flushing, Julie glanced down. Her toes, in brown knee socks, peeked oddly from beneath the taffeta skirt. She heard Mr. Lonsdale chuckle.

"Hello, Cinderella," he said.

There was a friendliness in the tall man's manner that put Julie unexpectedly at ease. She looked up, grinning, and shook her head. "The shoe didn't fit," she said. "I wear size seven and a half."

Mr. Lonsdale laughed heartily. "Well, anyway, you look quite attractive, Julie," he went on. "Doesn't she, Tom?"

For the first time Julie's eyes met her father's, darker than her own and momentarily reflected his deepest thoughts. He was looking at her and beyond her, back across the years. He wasn't seeing Julie in the dress; he was seeing another girl.

"It's a dress of Mother's," Julie told him, as though he didn't know. Then she stumbled on. "I was just—trying it on. Because I'm going to get a long dress for the party. I wanted to see how it would look." All Julie's temporary assurance—her courage to make a joke with Mr. Lonsdale—fled before the look in her father's eyes. She wanted to get upstairs and take the dress off quickly. She hadn't meant to make him remember so much.

But as Julie hesitated, her father snapped back to the present with a jerk. "Attractive?" he asked in reply to Mr. Lonsdale's question. "I'd say she looked a mite like a picked chicken, myself."

His tone was roughly affectionate, but Julie only heard the words, and though she had anticipated them, they made her feel hot all over. Her mother, she was sure, hadn't looked like a picked chicken in the dress. Her father's eyes had told her that. She had looked—lovely.

Julie's lashes dropped again, and she bit her lip. Gradually she began to edge along the cupboard toward the door. She was painfully aware of the damp garments clutched behind her back, and she avoided Mr. Lonsdale's eyes. "I'll go up and change," she murmured, then backed into the hall and started to tiptoe upstairs, as though by mere quietness she could erase the impression of her exit.

"Julie's growing up, Tom," she heard Mr. Lonsdale say. "You embarrassed her."

"Did I?" came her father's deep voice, lifting in surprise. "I didn't mean to. Julie's a funny kid. Shy. Not a bit like Margaret."

Tears of humiliation filled Julie's eyes. So her father felt he had to apologize for her. Not a bit like Margaret! Dimly as she remembered her mother, Julie knew it was true. Mother had never been self-conscious or ill at ease. She'd had a warm way of looking at people, a light way of laughing. Mother had never been *shy*.

Julie pulled the dragging dress to her knees as she fled up the third-floor stairs. She dropped the damp underwear on the staircase post and jerked the full-skirted gown over her head. Folding it hastily, she put it back in its place in the blanket chest, tucking in around it the muslin sheet that had been its dust cover.

"Not a bit like Margaret." The words echoed in her brain. She'd never be able to find, for the money her father had promised, the party dress that would make a new Julie Ferguson of her. Dick wouldn't ask her to dance, and even if he did, she'd be bound to stumble all over his feet. As for conversation—even if she knew the rules by heart, which she didn't—she'd be tongue-tied. It would be an awful party. Because she wasn't a bit like Margaret. She was a funny kid. Shy.

Resentfully, Julie picked up the overnight bag for which she had originally come to the attic, and blew at the dust on it. From the open stairwell she could hear Mr. Lonsdale's voice clearly coming up from the hall. "I'm looking for the best litter Scarlet's ever had. If only I could have put off this European trip—"

Julie set the bag down quietly on the top step and went over to put on her sweater and skirt. She didn't look in the mirror again: she walked quickly back to the windowsill she had deserted and curled up with her knees under her chin.

5

Scarlet, left unleashed in the yard, was standing by the fence gazing calmly down toward the brook, where two cows were drinking. The late afternoon sunlight was soft over the farm, graying the greenish yellow of the fields. The maple by the yard gate had red buds on it.

Little by little, Julie's troubled feeling slipped away. She sat for a long time on the windowsill, watching Scarlet, and she could almost feel her mood change. Her hot face cooled; the tight muscles of her stomach relaxed; the ache in her throat disappeared. She could forget the scene downstairs as though it had never happened, because Scarlet was there.

Just to watch the collie turn her head gave Julie a sharp sense of delight. She'd make a wonderful picture—gold and white against that green. Unconsciously the girl narrowed her eyes.

Some artist should paint her. Mother could have done it. I'd like to try, Julie thought.

But as soon as the idea took shape, Julie pushed it away from her. Someday, when she was older, after she had studied at the Academy, after she had really learned to paint. Then, perhaps; but not now. She could remember a time, in third grade, when she'd tried to draw Dick Whittington's cat. She could see the cat! She'd known exactly how he should look. But when she had tried to get him down on paper she couldn't do it. The teacher had praised her drawing, had said, "You have a real knack with a pencil," but Julie had shaken her head. That wasn't Dick's cat at all. A ghost of a smile touched her lips as she thought how any efforts of hers would distort Scarlet's magnificence. No, she wouldn't dare try to draw her now.

Julie sat for a long time on the windowsill, until the sun had dropped behind the hill where the barn stood, until the Lonsdale car had eased its way across the brook bridge and climbed the steep rise to the road. She watched her father lead the collie toward the barn, saw his lips move as he spoke to her. His voice would be gentle, Julie knew. He would be letting Scarlet know she could trust him. Tom Ferguson, people always said, was a man who understood dogs.

With the sun withdrawn from the glass, the window recess was getting cold. Julie drew the sleeves of her sweater down over her forearms and pulled herself back to the immediate present. It was getting late. The underwear was still not dry. There was supper to get, her hair to wash, her homework. With an exaggerated sigh she unwound her legs and stepped back to the floor. At the same moment her father's voice boomed up the stairwell.

"Julie!"

"Yes, Dad." An awareness of the passing of time settled on Julie as she hurried downstairs. Tom Ferguson, standing in the kitchen doorway, was eying the empty stove.

"Where have you been, Julie?"

"In the attic. Getting the overnight bag." The imminence of the Freshman Frolic swept over her in a high-riding wave and her throat felt tight again.

"Overnight bag?"

"Saturday's the freshman party. I'm going to spend the weekend with Anne." It seemed incredible to Julie that her dad could have forgotten.

"Oh." The word was little more than a grunt, but it signified recollection.

Julie glanced at the clock. Her father was a man of regular habits, and when he was hungry he could take it into his head to blame the party for his impatience. "I'll hurry supper. The potatoes are all peeled. I didn't think—"

"Didn't think!" Her father bit at the words. "Julie, you've got to start thinking. I know it's not easy for you, without a housekeeper here. But Mrs. Mott does come in mornings. You only have our suppers."

"I'm sorry." Julie didn't mean to sound grudging. She was really sorry because she knew her dad was swamped with spring work at the farm and the hour of daylight after the evening meal was valuable to him. But somehow the words came out wrong.

"It's this daydreaming," her father went on. "This—this mooning around. You started upstairs when Mr. Lonsdale was here. It couldn't have taken an hour to find the bag." His bristling eyebrows were almost meeting over his deep-set eyes as he tried to justify his irritation. "When there are things to be done, you can't afford to fool around. You've got to develop some sense of responsibility."

Julie was at the stove, her back to her father. "I said I was sorry, Dad," she repeated, and this time her voice was softer. "I—I got to

7

watching the collie instead of the time."

At mention of the dog the man's forehead smoothed out. "She's a handsome animal."

"Beautiful," Julie breathed, and now she could almost smile. Looking up from the bread she was slicing she asked, "Is she going to stay long?"

"Two or three months. She's about due to give birth."

This Julie already knew. "Pups are fun in the spring," she said, and her knife paused midway through a slice of bread as she got to thinking about them.

"These pups will be gold-edged," her father went on, pleased by increasing evidence that supper was on its way. "Scarlet's the best of the Lonsdale dogs, and she's been bred to a Scottish champion." He took his can of tobacco down from the shelf by the door and stuffed tobacco into the bowl of his pipe, punching it down with his index finger. "I was thinking, for the first few weeks, we might keep the pups in the house."

"We could rig up a bed for them right here in the kitchen, where it's warm," Julie agreed.

She flung a cloth over the pine table and clattered back and forth from the cupboard with dishes and silver, relieved that her father's attention was deflected from herself. He was tipping backward on a straight chair, now, balancing his hundred and eighty pounds on two of its legs. Smoking thoughtfully, he waited several minutes before he spoke.

"There's a big packing box in the barn. I guess that's the thing to do."

But Julie's mind, meanwhile, had raced off. If her dad had forgotten that this was the weekend of the party, mightn't that mean he had also forgotten the money for the dress? The dress was all-important. She *had* to have it. And she couldn't think of anything else—not even of Scarlet's anticipated puppies—until she was sure about it.

"Dad, you know the money for the dress you promised me—"

"Dress?" His boots stretched out before him, his pipe hissing away, he had seemed relaxed and approachable, but now he drew his eyebrows downward.

"Oh, Dad, you *know*." It simply wasn't possible that he could have forgotten the money. "The long dress. For the party I'm on the decorating committee for. I told you a month ago and you promised. Anne and her mother are going to shop with me." The words rushed out in a worried gush.

"If I promised, that's that. What'll you need?"

"Seventy dollars," Julie gulped out. She knew that cash was always scarce in the spring, but this time she couldn't help it. This had to be a really nice dress. Maybe Scarlet's coming to board would help.

"Is a long dress something you'll wear a lot?" Julie noticed her father's eyes on the hole worn clear through the elbow of her sweater as he asked the question. His voice was mild and a little confused. It occurred to Julie suddenly that he must find it puzzling to bring up a daughter, and she grinned when she answered.

"I probably won't wear it much at all. But I've *got* to have it."

Tom Ferguson looked directly at his daughter for several seconds, then rose and walked out of the room. Julie, as she mashed the potatoes with a wire beater, was in an agony of suspense. It seemed ages before he came back, unfolding seven rumpled ten-dollar bills that he held in his left hand.

"Here you are."

"Oh, thanks!" Julie's voice was weak with relief, and she accepted the money as though it were a fortune.

Her father looked down at her curiously. "In return will you do something for me?"

Already Julie had forgotten the earlier lecture. "Sure, Dad. What?"

"Try to keep your wits about you."

Julie bit her lip and flushed. She nodded. "I really will try, Dad."

"And Julie—"

Julie looked up.

"I'm sorry if I—well, if I embarrassed you this afternoon."

"That's all right." Julie's candid brown eyes bore no ill will. "I did look sort of like a—picked chicken, I guess."

Tom Ferguson patted his daughter on the shoulder awkwardly. "You'll fill out," he said. "And now can we eat?"

After supper Julie packed her bag. She was excited in a way that made her hands cold and trembly, and as she tucked the seventy dollars into a side flap of the suitcase and pinned it securely, she began thinking about the dress again. Tomorrow afternoon she and Anne were to meet Mrs. Sawyer, Anne's mother, after school. They could shop until five, Mrs. Sawyer explained. Then, if they found nothing suitable, they'd have all day Saturday left.

It seemed thrilling to Julie to be staying in town for a long weekend. Especially at the Sawyers'. Anne stood for all the things Julie wanted to be. Her hair curled and her skin was like pale cream, not sugared with freckles like Julie's. She was sure of herself and she knew when to talk and when to keep quiet. The boys liked her.

Carefully, Julie refolded her one whole pair of pajamas and laid them carefully on top of her slip. The pajamas were striped cotton, but they would have to do. Tomorrow night would be fun. She and Anne could talk in bed. Tomorrow night might be even more fun than Saturday. But now she could shake off that continuing dread about the dance. With a new dress, and being on the decorating committee and all, why shouldn't she have fun?

Why shouldn't she?

Now my hair, Julie thought, once the suitcase was packed. She shampooed it three times for good measure, and rinsed it again and again.

Friday's classes were never-ending.

Julie squirmed and fidgeted as the morning dragged. She wrote notes to Anne on torn scraps of paper.

"Do you think green or yellow? Or what about blue?"

And Anne wrote back.

"Not *blue!!!* Blue changes to dirty gray at night."

Julie discarded blue.

All the freshman girls were restless with excitement. It wasn't Julie alone. In the lunchroom at noon they could discuss nothing but what they were going to wear to the Frolic. Julie felt that being on the decorating committee gave her a certain obligation to offer advice. "I wouldn't wear red," she urged plump Sue Downs. "The decorations are going to be orange and green." Then, when Sue wailed in a stricken voice, "But red's all I've got!" she felt dreadful, and tried to take back her words, though she knew the damage had been done.

Nobody discussed boys. For one thing, the lunchroom was too public, and for another, boys weren't the most important thing right now. Julie pushed aside her empty bowl of cream of tomato soup and drew toward her the plate that held a big chunk of chocolate cake. Sue, nibbling at a salad in an eleventh-hour excess of concern about her pudginess, watched her enviously, but Julie didn't notice. She was listening to the conversation of the other girls.

"Mother says you ought to dress to suit your type," Anne was saying with conviction. "She says I should wear white and pastels, never heavy, bright colors." Without actually bragging, she was making the group at the table conscious of her china-doll prettiness.

Julie wondered what Mrs. Sawyer might consider her type to be. It worried her.

"My mother," Sidney Burns cut in, "always lets me choose my own clothes." Sidney was a big girl with large teeth and a hearty laugh. She wasn't, Julie thought, in the least pretty, but she knew how to handle herself and she generally managed to have the last word. As usual, the remark commanded a certain respect.

"She does? Lucky you!" Connie Blake, the youngest of the three Blake girls who lived in a sprawling old house on High Street, looked sincerely envious. Then her eyes began to twinkle, and she giggled infectiously. "Now me. I wear first Mary's hand-me-downs, then Pat's. I always tell Mother it's like having a secondhand skin."

Julie looked at Connie in considerable wonder. Most girls would never have admitted such a problem, much less have laughed about it. But Connie's eyelashes were long and black, and they curled back from blue eyes that held no hint of deceit. Connie would have fun at the party, no matter what she wore. Julie envied her. She wished she could be like that—happy-go-lucky. Instead of *wanting* things so desperately.

"I'm going to fix my hair a new way," Anne continued. Immediately Julie could see that half the other girls at the table considered the possibility of also styling their hair differently. "There's a picture in one of Mother's magazines of the neatest style!"

Julie finished her chocolate cake and patted at the crumbs with her fork. She went back to wondering about her type.

The first bell rang and the lunchroom began to empty. Julie would have liked to walk upstairs with Anne, but Sidney got there first. "There's something I've simply got to tell you!" the big girl said in an elaborate stage whisper that made the secret something so infinitely fascinating that Julie could scarcely resist joining them. But she knew, if she did, that Sidney would shut up like a clam. Sidney didn't consider that Julie quite belonged, lately.

In lots of ways, Julie realized, as she trailed along with Sue Downs, the crowd was narrowing down. In grammar school there had been a big group—fifteen or more—and eligibility had meant only the ability to be a good sport, play a fair game of this or that, and follow the general pattern of behavior. But now things were getting more complicated. For some reason Sidney and Anne and some of the other girls seemed to be growing away from Julie. Even when she tried, it was hard for her to put her finger on how this was being done. There were just a lot of little things—a difference in the way the girls walked, a new shrillness to their voices when any of the boys happened within earshot. Anne had run for secretary of the freshman class and had been elected. At meetings, Julie watched in astonishment the calmness with which she walked to the front of the room and marveled at the steadiness of her voice as she read the minutes. She herself could never have managed it. She would have died of embarrassment. But then, of course, she never would have been nominated. That was all part of the change.

More and more, Julie felt that she was sitting on the sidelines, watching the more popular girls grow up and away from her. Sometimes she was sick with jealousy. At other times she was simply resentful. First she would blame herself, knowing that she was neither as pretty as Anne nor as amusing as Connie, nor did she have Sidney's gift for small talk. Then again she would hate the girls for trying to rush her into feeling that boys and clothes and such things were so important. She would be seized with a breathless desire to get away, to be alone. I need more time, she kept thinking—more time to grow up.

In the first floor hall Julie picked up her history book and Latin grammar from the rack where she had parked them and wandered into her first afternoon class. It was a comfort, at any rate, to know that this weekend the mere fact she was staying at Anne's house would make her a part of things. She rather wondered, however, why Anne had asked her. They hadn't been nearly so friendly, this year, as in the past. It couldn't be, could it, that Anne had extended the invitation because she felt a little sorry for her?

Deliberately, Julie put such an idea out of her mind. Anne and she had known each other since they were babies, practically—since the days long before Mother had died and she and Dad had moved out to the farm. The friendship of their parents dated back even farther than that. Ella Emmons and Margaret Field had gone to art school together in Philadelphia when they were girls, before they acquired the married names of Sawyer and Ferguson. It was the most natural thing in the world that Mrs. Sawyer should want to help Julie choose a dress, and that Anne should ask her to stay in for the weekend.

Shirley Graham, chairman of the decorating committee, bustled in from the hall and, spotting Julie, came over to her desk. "Can you be at the gym at nine tomorrow morning, Julie? There's so much to be done we're going to have to start early." She sounded as though she were full of responsibilities.

"I think so." Julie added, "I'm spending the weekend with Anne."

Shirley was comparatively new to Meadowbrook, having transferred from a city school only the year before. She knew nothing of the background of Julie and Anne's friendship, and Julie could see her eyes widen a little in surprise. She could tell that she'd gone up a notch in Shirley's estimation, because the girl settled down on the desk in front of hers and said, conversationally, "What are you going to wear tomorrow night?"

"I don't know yet," Julie admitted. Then she said, casually, "I'm shopping for a dress this afternoon."

"Oh! Fun!" Shirley gushed, and would have said more, but Miss Durham had entered the room and was trying to quiet the confusion so that she could start class. " 'Bye, now." Shirley walked away.

Julie sat and stared out the window. Then she made a diligent effort to get the idea of what Miss Durham was saying. The effort was too great and the subject was too dull, so she gave up and stared out the window again. It was like that all afternoon.

Finally three o'clock came. Julie was at the door before Anne, her books stowed in her locker and her overnight bag clutched in her hand. Outside, in the car, Mrs. Sawyer was waiting. At last the weekend was really going to begin!

"Hi, Mom!" Anne opened the door for Julie.

"Hello, Mrs. Sawyer."

"Hello, girls. Hurry and climb in. I'm blocking traffic." Dodging a number of jaywalking high-school students, Mrs. Sawyer started off downtown.

"Now, let's see. I have some errands to do, but Julie's dress is the first thing," she chirped. Julie could never think of her as anything but birdlike. She had her daughter's fair hair and skin, but she was more petite and much more rapid in her speech and movements. Her hair

14

and clothes were becoming. Julie thought she had style.

"What about the Corner Shop?" Anne suggested. Her dress had come from there.

Julie thought she might as well come out with it bluntly. "I have seventy dollars to spend," she said. It had seemed like a lot, last night. Now it seemed like a little. "Only," she added.

Mrs. Sawyer considered. "Well, we might try the Elite first. Though it would be just luck if we found anything there. Then there's that new little shop down around the corner from the library. Of course Meadowbrook isn't Philadelphia."

Julie looked concerned.

"But goodness knows," Mrs. Sawyer hurried on, "we'll be able to find something you like. Anne did. And as for the money, seventy dollars is plenty to put into a party dress for a girl your age."

Julie's face brightened and she let out a long breath of relief.

There was nothing suitable in the store called the Elite. Mrs. Sawyer whisked Julie and Anne in and out of the place with scant ceremony. Julie was increasingly glad that she had the guidance of her friend's mother, because, for her own part, she had thought some of the dresses the salesgirl had brought out were beautiful—especially a pale-pink organdy with roses on the skirt.

On the way to the Corner Shop she murmured, timidly, "That pink organdy . . ."

But Mrs. Sawyer would have none of it. "Sleazy material," she pronounced. "And too old for a high-school freshman."

In the Corner Shop the salesclerk was so smartly dressed that she frightened Julie, but Anne and her mother smiled and spoke to her casually. "And do you like your dress as well as when you bought it, dear?" the woman asked Anne. "You should, because you look perfectly adorable in it, with those yellow curls."

Mrs. Sawyer drew Julie forward, and the salesclerk glanced at her for the first time. "Today, Miss Moore, we're looking for something for this young lady."

Julie felt very conscious that the sleeves of her coat were too short. Secretly she tried to pull them down, avoiding Miss Moore's eyes.

"Something in a party dress?"

Mrs. Sawyer nodded. "Something very simple." She turned to

Julie. "Slip off your coat, dear." Then back to Miss Moore. "Size 8?"

Miss Moore nodded. "I'll see what we have."

To Julie's surprise, she returned with four dresses over her arm. The first was a flowered fabric containing all the colors of spring. "I think that's beautiful!" Julie breathed, her eyes aglow.

But Mrs. Sawyer shook her head. "Not on you, dear. On Anne, perhaps. But your coloring would be all wrong for it."

Julie flushed. She felt that the freckles across the bridge of her nose were shining like new pennies.

Miss Moore shook out a white dress. "Now that's nice," Mrs. Sawyer said. "You might try that on."

"But my dress is white," Anne objected.

"That wouldn't matter," said Mrs. Sawyer. But Julie knew it would.

The third dress was pink, and Julie, thinking of the freckles, anticipated that Mrs. Sawyer would shake her head. The fourth was a plaid cotton, with eyelet embroidery around the neck and puffed sleeves, run through with velvet ribbon. There was deep blue in it, and a rust red, and a lot of tan and white.

Mrs. Sawyer took the dress from the clerk and held it against Julie. "That's perfect with your coloring," she said.

While she was getting out of her sweater and skirt, in the fitting room, the fact that it was cotton bothered Julie. It didn't make it seem like a party dress. Cotton was something she had worn half her life. But when she got the dress over her head and the full skirt fell in a wide sweep to the floor, when Miss Moore had run up the zipper so that the dress hugged her slim waist, when she had shaken her hair out over her shoulders and perked up the full sleeves, she began to see what Mrs. Sawyer meant. The dress was right on her, somehow.

The color of her hair was exactly the same bright tan as the plaid. The same color, Julie thought momentarily, as the sable in Scarlet's coat. She felt very far away from the farm and from the collie at this moment. She wondered what Scarlet and her dad were doing. Then she walked out of the fitting room to show Mrs. Sawyer the dress.

"That's very good on you, Julie," Mrs. Sawyer nodded at once. "Just right with your hair and eyes. Turn around." Julie turned. "A perfect fit. Did you look at the price?"

16

The dress was $63.95.

While it was being wrapped Julie looked toward the white dress with a certain amount of longing, but by the time they left the shop she felt quite satisfied. For her remaining six dollars, and five that Julie herself had saved from her birthday, Mrs. Sawyer suggested that they might be able to find a pair of blue sandals that would match the blue in the dress. Julie had forgotten all about shoes. She agreed at once. And finally, the sandals bought and Mrs. Sawyer's shopping completed, they got into the car and drove home.

Julie always loved staying at the Sawyers'. The house was comfortable and gay, with bright slipcovering on the living room furniture and flowers and candles on the dining room table. To Julie, coming back from the farm to a house like this was like entering another world. While she was usually too shy to participate, she enjoyed the family conversation and the confusion caused by Anne's younger brother and sister.

After dinner she and Anne went upstairs to spread out and admire each other's dresses. Then Julie tried on Anne's and Anne tried on Julie's. Finally they turned on the small clock radio by Anne's bed and sat on the floor with a manicuring set, doing their nails. They talked constantly, then and later, after they were settled in bed with the lights out. A full moon shone on the white pillows, and they rested on their elbows, whispering and giggling. Mrs. Sawyer knocked twice on their door, first in warning that was mild and understanding, then firmly.

"No more talking. It's eleven o'clock. Go to sleep, girls."

But even after Anne was deep in slumber Julie lay awake. She was filled with an inner excitement that made her capable of extraordinary things. She could see herself at the party, lively in the plaid dress, popular. Not only Dick, but lots of the other boys wanted to dance with her. She was able to think of the cleverest things to say! She was the Julie Ferguson she *felt*, not the one she seemed to other people. It was very gratifying to be a success. It was very . . . pleasant . . . indeed.

Of course the next morning none of the night thoughts were real. Julie ate breakfast hastily and rushed off to the high school to work on the decorations while Anne, as a concession to the importance of the

17

occasion, went grandly off to the hairdresser's.

The decorations didn't please Julie. To her artistic eye the color scheme was cheap and brash. But she worked at decorating the gym eagerly, and the occasional ideas she offered were generally adopted. She hummed happily from the top of her stepladder. She was having a good time.

When Julie got back to the Sawyers' Anne was sitting at the desk in the hall, just replacing the telephone in its cradle.

"Hi!" Julie grinned, feeling smudged and untidy but very much part of things.

"What do you think!" Anne announced in a tone of delighted surprise. "Chunky Spencer just asked if he could take me to the party."

Julie's heart dropped to her stomach and lay there, heavy and soggy. "Oh, Anne, that's nice!" She stretched her mouth in a smile. Why hadn't she anticipated this? Why had she been so dumb? Anne was one of the prettiest of the freshman girls, and Chunky had been pausing at her homeroom desk quite often lately. It was just that so few of their crowd had actual dates, only the very most popular. And Anne had said so offhandedly, "Daddy will drive us in the car."

"Of course you can go with us," Anne went on. "I told Chunky you were here for the weekend."

"Thanks, but I have to go early anyway. On account of the decorations," Julie replied.

Then a really horrible thought swept her. What about coming home? She wouldn't walk home with Chunky and Anne. She would not! But even worse would be to drag Mr. Sawyer out with the car to come for her alone. Her hands turned cold with panic. She'd have to think of some way out!

"I'm dirty as the dickens," Julie said, looking down at her hands. "Can I take a bath?"

"Sure. There's plenty of time before dinner."

Julie hurried upstairs.

She could pretend to be sick, and leave in the middle of the evening. She could buttonhole Dick and just lay her cards on the table and say—what could she say? She could hope that at the last minute somebody would call and ask her for a date, too. But she knew that nobody would. She wished she had stayed at the farm. Then Dick *might* have offered to stop by for her; they lived so close. But she had told him last week she was staying in town with Anne.

Water rushing from the bathroom tap seemed a proper accompaniment for her state of mind. She didn't turn off the faucet until she had to. Anne was singing a popular song in her bedroom. She always knew all the words. In the middle of a phrase she broke off to call: "I've got some new nail polish, Julie. It's a luscious shade. You can use some if you want."

"Thanks, Anne. I'd love to," Julie called back. She squeezed the water out of her washcloth and held it with both hands over her face.

Clinging to the inside edge of the pavement, Julie sped along the suburban streets. The skirt of her dress almost brushed the sidewalk, and she had to hold it up in front to keep from tripping. She felt a little foolish, in the late dusk—to be out alone, and in a party outfit. But not so foolish as she would have felt walking to the party with Chunky and Anne.

Fortunately, the excuse about the decorations had worked. Mr. Sawyer, stretched out in his lounge chair after dinner, was easily persuaded that no harm could come to Julie on her way to the school, since it was not yet dark. And the reason that she must go early had been accepted unsuspiciously by Mrs. Sawyer, who was concerned only about the girls' getting home.

"Chunky will bring us," said Anne.

"I'll come for you in the car," corrected her father.

"Oh, Daddy, no! I'll look like a baby!"

"You are a baby," retorted Mr. Sawyer. "Now, no argument, Anne."

Anne flounced upstairs and fumed the entire time she was dressing. "Now what'll I ever tell Chunky?" she demanded of Julie.

Julie was too preoccupied to be of much comfort. "I guess you'll just have to tell him the truth."

The evening air was damp and fresh and full of promise. The long fronds of a forsythia bush, showing faintly yellow in the dusk, brushed Julie's coat as she hurried along. A car horn honked, and a black sedan slowed beside the curb. She noticed it, but kept her eyes straight in front and walked even faster. Then a familiar voice called: "Julie Ferguson! Want a lift?"

It was only Doc Harper, the vet.

Julie stopped and turned. "No, thanks, Doctor. I'm not in a hurry." Then she flushed as she realized that her pace had contradicted her words.

"Okay." The doctor must have seen her party dress. "I was just on my way out to your place. That's why I stopped."

Julie's curiosity made her repeat, "Out to our place?" Scarlet flashed into her mind. She moved closer to the car.

The ruddy-faced veterinarian nodded as he let out his clutch. "A collie your father's boardin'. . . ." he called back, but the rest of his sentence was lost.

That's it, Julie decided, as she started on slowly. Scarlet must be having her pups.

The high school still looked deserted when Julie reached it. The corridors smelled of chalk and long-used books and stale clothing. A janitor with a cleaning brush and a long-handled dustpan smiled at her, although he didn't know her name.

"Tonight's the big night, eh?"

He looked at her so kindly that Julie had to smile back. "I guess it is."

She met a couple of boys in the hall leading to the gym. They came from outlying country districts, like herself, and rode the same school bus. Julie hastened past them importantly. "Hi," she said in progress. "Seen any of the decorating committee around?"

The boys stared at her. "Unh-unh," one of them said, not understanding her meaning.

The girls' locker room was entirely vacant, and Julie was in no hurry to take off her coat. She walked around behind the second row of metal cabinets, and waited until a fair-sized crowd had arrived. Then, as though she were just returning from depositing something in her own locker, she emerged.

Girls, noisy and smelling of perfume, crowded in front of the single oak-bordered mirror, above which hung a 40-watt bulb. Seen in a glimpse over a ruffled shoulder, Julie's own reflection looked misty and unreal. A sense of anticipation began to seep into her again.

It grew as the room became crowded. Julie mingled with the girls, talking to her friends, admiring their dresses, modestly dismissing her

21

own. She combed her hair again and put on lipstick. Every time the door opened the clamor increased, and then the laughter and talk became mingled with music, and groups of the girls began deserting the locker room for the decorated gym.

To enter the gym, Julie attached herself to Connie Blake. Because Connie never seemed self-conscious, Julie felt comparatively safe by her side. A stereo had been connected to a loudspeaker, and there was a scratch and thump as one tune ended and another began. The Freshman Frolic had officially begun.

It wasn't at all as Julie had expected. Nobody acted as though the party was very much fun except a couple of boys who were making mock tackles at each other and howling uproariously. The girls stood about in little knots, looking scrubbed and shining but slightly uncomfortable in their long dresses. They didn't seem to know what to do with their hands.

Julie, in Connie's wake, joined one of the groups, which included Sidney and little Sue Downs, brave and pudgy in her red dress. Julie made a conscious effort and said, "You look sweet, Sue!"

Boys were talking to other boys, standing around the record player. Their voices were shrill with excitement and many of them wore sport coats. They were very conscious of the girls' long dresses, but pretended not to be.

Julie saw Anne come into the gym in front of Chunky. Like the other girls who had "dates," Anne had managed to arrive rather late. A very few couples were dancing, and several girls were trying to get up courage to dance together, hoping that then some of the boys would cut in. Everybody else was just standing around.

Mr. Pennypacker, the faculty adviser, was consulting Miss Miller, the chaperone. They were nodding their heads, agreeing on something. A few minutes later Julie found out what it was. They were going to start a circle dance.

"That's a good idea," said Connie Blake. "Come on, Julie. Come on, Sue." She spread her arms and took their hands. Almost all the other girls joined them, making a big ring in the middle of the floor. But persuading the boys to participate wasn't easy. Some came readily enough, but others hung back, waiting to be coaxed or claiming they didn't dance. In the end the leftover girls had to count off, and every second one had to take a boy's place.

The whistle blew and the dance started. Julie danced first with Gordon Wyatt, a tall boy with glasses who joined in every sport with solemn determination. He danced that way now, carefully, without speaking.

"You're a good dancer," Julie said.

"Thank you," Gordon replied.

Until the whistle blew again this was the extent of their conversation.

Next Julie danced with one of the girls. She didn't mind, now, because Anne, dancing with another girl, too, was smiling and acting as though it were fun. Julie smiled and began to relax. Dick Webster passed her and grinned. "Hi, Peanut," he called. The nickname made Julie feel at home.

But the circle dance ended too soon. The girls drifted back to the sidelines and the boys retired to their territory around the record player. Only a few couples remained in the middle of the room and started to dance. The boys on the edge of things watched them and made loud comments. There was a good deal of horseplay. But gradually the ice was broken, and more and more of the boys came sliding across the floor to ask the girls to dance. At other times, boys cut in on two girls dancing together. That was all right, Julie thought, if you weren't the girl who was left in the middle of the floor, to march back to the wall unescorted. She decided she wouldn't take the chance.

Once her heart leaped as Dick skated across the floor in her direction, but he came up short before Connie, and bowed elaborately, clowning for her. Julie followed the pair nervously, tapping her foot. She wished somebody would ask her to dance.

Finally someone did. It was Gordon Wyatt again. He danced so stiffly that Julie was sure the group on the sidelines must be laughing at the pair of them. She couldn't think of a word to say and she even forgot to smile. Gordon returned her to the cluster of girls fidgeting on the edge of the basketball court with little comment.

Julie escaped to the locker room and combed her hair once more, taking a long time about it. Five or six of the least attractive girls in the freshman class were grouped around the mirror, also stalling for time. As Julie was finishing, Anne and Connie, arm in arm, banged through

23

the door, and Julie had to face the humiliation of being found among them.

For Anne and Connie were birds of a different feather from the group hiding out in the locker room. They were flushed and laughing, talking about the boys loudly.

"Isn't Johnny Powell a scream?"

"You know, Gordon Wyatt's really awfully nice, in a quiet sort of way."

Then they saw Julie.

"Hi, Julie! What are you doing here? Come on out and have some fun." The words classified the other girls cruelly, and gave Julie the benefit of the doubt.

"You were just dancing with Gordon, Julie. He's not bad, is he?"

"No, he's not bad." Why had she been so silly as to have imagined people were laughing at her? Why had she become tongue-tied? Now she knew for a certainty that Gordon wouldn't ask her to dance again.

Julie followed Anne and Connie back to the gym. As they entered the door, Chunky detached himself from a group of boys and grabbed Anne's hand, and a short, freckle-faced lad who had not yet ventured out on the floor planted himself before Connie.

"D-dance?" he stammered.

"Sure, Billy." Connie wrinkled her nose and grinned at Julie as he whirled her away.

Julie, left alone, had a moment of panic. She could rejoin the huddle of girls against the wall or she could beat a retreat back to the locker room. Then a familiar voice made her whirl around.

"Dance, Peanut?"

"Dick! Oh, thanks!"

Then, realizing what the relief in her tone had admitted, Julie flushed beet red.

Dick laughed. He had a nice laugh—hearty and teasing. It went with his square jaw and wide-set blue eyes and his rather large mouth. "What's the matter, small fry? Were you stuck?"

Julie, recovering herself, bristled. "I just that moment came in from the locker room."

Dick laughed again.

I've got to make him stop treating me like the kid next door, Julie

24

kept thinking as they worked their way around the floor. Dick was far from skillful with his feet and it took considerable concentration to follow him at all, but even so Julie felt she must make the effort. Talk and laugh—that's what the other girls were doing. Talk and laugh. But about what?

Taking a deep breath, Julie plunged.

"Nice party, isn't it?"

Dick shrugged.

"D'you like to dance?"

"Not much."

Julie grinned determinedly. These conversational dead ends were alarming. There must be something she could chatter on about.

"Y'know, Dick, Mr. Lonsdale brought another collie out to board on Thursday. She's simply beautiful! Sable and white, with the loveliest coat. Dad says she's one of the handsomest dogs Mr. Lonsdale has ever bred."

Dick grunted.

"Her name's Scarlet," Julie raced on, "and she's going to have puppies any minute. Maybe she's having them now. I met Doc Harper on the way down here, and he was on his way out to our place." She paused for breath.

Dick was following Connie Blake with his eyes. He hadn't heard a word she'd said. "Y'know, Peanut, that Blake gal's got something," he muttered. "Look at her making little Billy Bowen think he's six foot two."

Julie looked, and bit her lip. It was no use. She hadn't the technique; she hadn't the personality; she hadn't anything. For the rest of her life, she supposed, she'd be stranded on the outskirts. She simply didn't belong.

Dick, she thought dejectedly, was just the same as always. He hadn't changed. Or not much, anyway. But the girls had changed. The girls had changed completely. They had a new way about them that the boys liked—that is, the popular girls like Anne and Connie did. And what that way was Julie couldn't figure out. Her set smile faded and she stumbled unexpectedly.

"Hey there!" Dick yanked her upright.

"Sorry!" Injury seemed added to insult. Julie felt like saying: "That was your fault!" She would have said it—a year ago. But those days were gone.

Suddenly she wanted them back again, desperately. The long sun-dappled mornings in the tree house, the lazy afternoons at the dam. Dick, teaching her to dive, persistent yet patient. Dick, trading a particularly rare grasshopper with her, and pressing a shrewd deal.

Trading grasshoppers. Kid stuff. What a thing to be thinking about in the middle of the Freshman Frolic! No wonder she'd never be a social success.

The record was ending. The stereo would soon begin to scratch and thump, its labor magnified by the loudspeaker as the tune changed. Dick was steering her back to the cluster of long skirts near the locker room door.

"Thanks, Ju. 'Bye now," he said.

"Dick!" Julie clutched at his arm, realizing that a hope she had nourished in the back of her mind all evening was about to die a final death.

"Yeh?" His eyes were already searching the field, and he turned back to her absentmindedly.

"I'm staying at Anne's, you know. Anne came with Chunky Spencer." Julie swallowed her pride and raced on. "I thought—maybe—you'd like to ride back to Anne's with us. After the party, I mean."

"Who—me?" Dick looked astonished. "What'd I want to go back to Anne's for? I live in the other direction, remember? And I got the promise of a ride home."

He was gone, back into the swarm of boys around the stereo, and Julie was again alone.

Anne brushed past her just then. She was giggling at something Chunky had just said. Out of the corner of her eye she saw Julie and waved.

"Having a good time?" she called brightly.

"Wonderful!" Julie replied, and she put the required smile back on her face.

From then on, for the rest of the long weekend, all Julie wanted was to get back to the farm. She kept smiling and saying, "Wonderful!" when anybody spoke of the party, but inside she was sick.

One ordeal seemed to tread on the heels of another. First there was the major nightmare of riding home from the Frolic on the front seat of the car beside Mr. Sawyer while Chunky and Anne rode in the back. Then there was the necessity of keeping up a front when Anne, her party dress flung over a chair, settled down in bed with a contented sigh and whispered into the dark, "Now let's talk!" Finally there was a Sunday afternoon get-together of all the girls in the crowd on the Blakes' back porch. Everybody was overflowing with things to talk about except Julie. For her it was the most painful kind of torture.

School, Monday, was some relief. When Julie parked her overnight bag in the locker she thanked Anne profusely, as she had thanked her mother, for the Sawyer hospitality. But actually she was glad to be back in classes, where things followed a routine pattern and she knew what to expect next. By afternoon, however, she could scarcely wait to get home. She wanted to shake all memory of the dance from her, to put it behind her with other disagreeable things that couldn't be helped.

The school bus seemed to crawl along the last mile of gravel road that led to the Fergusons' lane. It was an uninteresting enough lane—just a rutted path that led straight back over level ground to a line of trees three hundred yards off the road. The field on the left had been plowed, but on the right last winter's grass had just been burned off and the stubble was black and smelly. Yet as she jumped down from the high bus step, every inch of the ground looked good to Julie. She knew what lay beyond.

With the overnight bag banging against her legs, she hurried along the crown of the lane. When the path reached the trees it swung to the left and dropped abruptly down. It was at the turn that Julie paused. She leaned against the sagging fence and looked out over the farm, which lay in a saucerlike valley below her. Nothing was changed, yet everything looked fresh and enticing. Julie drew a deep breath.

Immediately below her was the brook, broad and calm, idling along beneath sycamores and willows, spanned by a rickety Dutch bridge. The curving lane crossed the bridge and led past the white plaster house up a short rise to the spacious barn. Two cows and a calf were grazing in the fenced-in field beyond the stream, and a line of ducks was waddling up from the water's edge. It all looked safe, hidden, protected. Julie sighed and her lips moved. "Hello, farm," she said.

It seemed incredibly good to be back. Julie wondered, as she walked down the path, swinging the bag, that she had ever wanted to get away. She was anxious to see her dad. She forgot his gruffness and his preoccupation with farm work and remembered only the pleasant things about him—the gentleness of his hands with animals, the heartiness of his occasional laughter.

Of course there was some danger that he, too, might ask about the dance. Then she would have to cover up her true feelings and say again, "I had a lovely time." But the chances were that her father would never think about the party. She'd hang the long dress in the very back of her closet. She'd get into her jeans and go up the brook to look for wildflowers. She'd slip back into the familiar life of the farm with no announcement, as though she had never spent the weekend away.

Pebbles, rattling ahead of her down the road, proclaimed her progress, but there was no sign of life at the house, Then, just as she reached the bridge, Julie saw the back of a black car parked beside the barn.

She knew that car. It was Doc Harper's. And she realized at once that something was wrong. It could be one of the cows, of course, but Julie thought instantly—Scarlet! And she didn't know what she feared.

At the yard gate she put down her bag, planning to go on up to the barn, but before she had taken a step the house door slammed and Tom Ferguson, unshaven and with eyes red from sleeplessness, came out.

28

"Oh, hello, Julie," he said.

"Dad, what's the matter?"

"The collie has a bad blood infection. I've been trying to reach Lonsdale." He jerked his head back briefly in the direction of the phone. His voice sounded flat and tired.

"Oh, I'm so sorry." Julie stood still in the lane while her father passed her. Her arms hung loose at her sides and she didn't know how to help.

She watched her dad's back until he had turned in at the barn door. Then she reached for her bag again and walked up to the house. Very quietly, as though she were entering a sick room, she opened the door and went upstairs. Still quietly, she started to unpack. Before she finished, the phone rang.

"Yes, Mr. Lonsdale," Julie found herself saying. "Dad called about Scarlet. He's up at the barn. I'll go get him."

"Is anything wrong?"

The voice on the other end of the wire was full of concern and Julie suddenly decided to break the news herself. Dad wanted her to take more responsibility. This was her chance. "Scarlet has a bad blood infection. Dad and Dr. Harper are with her now. I don't know much about it but Dad seems awfully worried." There. It was out.

A short silence greeted her words. Then Mr. Lonsdale said: "Don't call your father to the phone, Julie. Just give him a message from me. Tell him to do his best. If Tom Ferguson and the best vet in the county can't pull Scarlet through, I know no one can."

Julie put the receiver back on the hook of the old-fashioned oak phone box on the hall wall and for the first time she was conscious of a soft scrabbling noise coming from the direction of the kitchen. As she listened the noise increased, and with it came a sound like chickens cheeping. Julie walked to the kitchen door before she recognized its source. In a box by the gas range huddled Scarlet's tiny puppies, wailing weakly for food.

Crossing the room on tiptoe, Julie sank down on her knees beside the box. Curled close together on an old blanket were four sleek, rat-like puppies, appallingly pink and white. They were all shuddering a little, but only one was crying, as he pushed with his whip of a tail, trying to mount the heap.

"Eep-eep-eep," he yelled with his mouth open wide, like a hungry bird's. "Eep-eep-eep."

Julie pulled the blanket up closer around them but she didn't touch them. They were pitiful little creatures, big-headed and unappealing, but they were alive. The sense of their enormous need swept over Julie in a wave. "Poor babies," she whispered under her breath. "Your mother will get well. Really she will."

Leaving them, she went out to the barn to deliver her message. She stood in the doorway, and after the sunlight the barn was a vast cavern of blackness that she scarcely dared enter, and she repeated Mr. Lonsdale's words haltingly, fighting to remember precisely what he had said.

Then she went back to the house, where all the puppies were now cheeping lustily, and without quite realizing that she was doing it, she began to work an old, childish spell. She laid the table for supper and she put each dish, each fork and spoon, down carefully, with mathematical exactness. She peeled potatoes and made sure that not one tiny speck, not one eye, not one sliver of the brown skin remained. She measured coffee for the pot and her tablespoonfuls were exact, to the nearest possible grain. Because maybe, if she did everything right—if she did every last thing exactly right—Scarlet would get well.

But the clock hands crept round, the sun sank, and Julie couldn't go on playing the half-forgotten game forever. She had known for years now that wishing doesn't make things so. It was a stall against time, really—a desperate hope—that had made her try it. She stood, her cold hands clasped, her fingers aching, and gazed through the window toward the barn. Six o'clock. Soon now her father would come.

She mashed the potatoes and put the fried ham on the back of the stove. From the exhaustion of crying, the puppies had gone back to sleep. She walked from the stove to the window and back to the stove again. Six-thirty, and still her father hadn't come.

Julie sat down in the rocker and chewed the corner of her lower lip. If only there were something more she could do. The telephone rang and it was one of the girls who lived nearby, to ask about the history homework. Julie answered her automatically, attacked by a sense of unreality. She felt as though she were two different persons, the Julie who lived at the farm and the Julie the school crowd knew. Even in

30

the midst of such agonizing waiting she felt more confident of the first Julie. She felt at least she could deal with things out here, but at school she felt increasingly baffled and uncertain.

Seven o'clock. Julie stirred more milk into the drying potatoes, and stopped her spoon as she heard the unmistakable starting of a motor. In a few seconds Dr. Harper's car swayed slowly down the lane and across the bridge. She watched it until it had climbed the rise.

Even before the front door closed behind her dad she sensed the verdict. Scarlet had died.

Tom Ferguson stared down at his food and pushed the plate away. Julie understood. He felt beaten and sick. With his immense love of animals and his stern sense of responsibility, he was stricken by failure. Julie felt closer to him than ever before in her life.

She swallowed some dinner but made no effort to talk. The puppies were cheeping again now, frantically, yet only she seemed to hear them. "Can we do anything about the pups, Dad?" she finally asked.

Her father's eyes shifted slowly to the box by the stove. "Pity," he said dully, not answering Julie's question. "It was a fine litter."

Was? Julie instinctively questioned the past tense. "Can't we possibly raise them?"

The faintest flicker of interest crossed her father's eyes. "They're only three days old, Julie. I'm afraid we wouldn't have a chance."

She noticed that he had returned her "we." It gave her a sense of partnership. "But we could at least try!"

Julie didn't know that her voice became insistent. Going over to look down at the newborn puppies she still found them ratlike and repulsive. But she clung to the fact that they were hungrily anxious to live. Someday they could be long-limbed, thick-coated, and elegant, like their mother.

"Dad, we just can't let them die!"

Tom got up from his chair and came over to where Julie was standing. He reached down to pick up one of the creatures and it squealed instinctively in alarm. Julie watched him turn it over in his big hands, feeling the neck, the legs, stroking the sleek back with his index finger. "They've got the makings of fine pups," he said, almost to himself. "The ears and eyes are well placed. Seeing them in the nest like this, any collie man would value them."

31

Julie snatched at this. "Couldn't we bottle feed them?" she asked.

Tom shook his head. "Too young." He paused. "Only thing we could use would be an eyedropper."

"Shall I go see if I can find one? In the medicine closet?"

"You might," said Julie's father. "You might."

Her prize removed from a bottle of eye drops, Julie came downstairs to find Tom heating milk on the stove, and adding to it a carefully measured quantity of lime water.

"Better get the hot-water bottle, too," he told Julie, "and a couple of glass jars with tight caps. We'll fill them with water from the kettle and try to keep the pups warm overnight."

Julie raced on her errands. Then she boiled the dropper, to sterilize it, and watched her father feed the infants lukewarm milk which he tested on the inside of his wrist. It was a slow process, but the puppies swallowed greedily and Tom was patient. Finally all four were replaced in the snug bed Julie made for them in the center of the containers of hot water wrapped in old Turkish towels.

"There," she said with a sigh of satisfaction. "Now you'll be fine." Her eyes were shining with accomplishment and she had temporarily forgotten Scarlet.

"Don't get your hopes up, Julie," Tom Ferguson said. "It'll be a long haul and the chances are stacked against us." Then he sat down again with his daughter and told her exactly how the odds lay.

It was probable that the mother had already transmitted the infection, Julie learned. In such a case there wouldn't be even a hope of saving the offspring. Even if Scarlet's milk had been untainted, raising a puppy by hand was a long and discouraging process. Tom described how it was done.

"Every two hours, night and day, they have to be fed."

"We'll take turns!" Julie's desire to help was boundless. She was ready for anything. Overriding her father's gloom, she began to make plans. "First we can set the alarm clock in my room, then in yours." A bright thought struck her. "Maybe I shouldn't even go to school this week," she said.

But her father dashed her hopes. "You've got to go to school. And you can't miss too much sleep. We'll have to work things out."

Julie, washing the dishes, almost hummed. She felt necessary and full of responsibility to the puppies and to her father. It was a good feeling, and it lasted until she went to bed.

Julie's was the first stint—the midnight one. Then Tom would get up at two in the morning, and Julie would take over again at four. The midnight feeding wasn't bad. The sense of excitement triggered early in the evening carried her through. But at four Julie could scarcely drag herself out of bed, and the hungry puppies choked and gasped and wriggled in her unaccustomed hands. Her eyelids kept closing; her feet were cold; her head was heavy with sleep. When she finally crawled back into bed the dawn was breaking, but the bright light of adventure had gone out.

Night and day, every two hours.

It seemed to Julie, after a while, that the puppies ate incessantly. One feeding was no sooner over than the next one began. But Tom, schooled to patience, was encouraged. Two days on the dropper and the infants were still alive.

Then, on Thursday afternoon, when Julie came home from school with a four-ounce nursing bottle and the smallest nipple she could buy at a Meadowbrook drugstore, she found only three puppies in the box. Anxiously she went down to the springhouse where her father was working and he confirmed her fears with a nod. "Don't be upset, Julie. Remember, if we raise one, we'll be lucky. Only the strong can survive."

"Only the strong can survive." She kept hearing her father's words as she walked back up to the house. Her hands were clenched and her throat was tight with tears. It was a rotten law. She hated it. But she recognized it as a law nevertheless. She knew it was true. At school it was the same as on the farm. Only the pretty girls, the bright girls, the self-confident, seemed to get ahead. The weak ones sank into the background and were nothing. How, Julie wondered, did the strong come to be?

She went into the kitchen and crouched down by the puppies' box. They were already awake and working their paws, hungry for the next feeding. Julie put an extra portion of milk formula into the pan.

"You've got to be strong, understand?" she told them sternly. "Eat now!"

The puppies ate. By the end of the week the Fergusons were able to shift the three from the dropper to the bottle, and with the ability to suck at a nipple their appetites increased. Noticeably, day by day, their coats became less sleek and more fluffy, until they lost their ratlike appearance and began to look like round balls of fur.

Julie told the girls at school about the puppies, not because she thought they'd be especially interested, but because she wanted to use her charges as an excuse for drifting farther and farther away from the doings of the "crowd" and into the less confusing life at the farm. She sat through lunches with a determinedly dreamy expression and tried not to listen to the buzz of conversation around her.

"Let's go to the movies Saturday afternoon, Anne," she'd hear Connie Blake suggest. And Anne would reply, "We could ask Sidney, too." Never, anymore, "We could ask Julie."

Of course it didn't matter now. She had the puppies. It didn't really matter a bit. Neither did the Freshman Frolic matter, she tried to convince herself, yet she dated everything from the night of the dance. That she had been an obvious social failure she knew beyond a shadow of a doubt. She felt certain that the really popular girls, like Anne and Connie and Shirley, would never want to include her in their plans again. She hurried home after school to her puppies and maintained an assumed detachment from lunchroom conversations about boys. But actually she felt left out.

On the May day when the litter was six weeks old Dick Webster slid into the seat next to Julie's on the school bus. "Hi, Peanut," he said.

"Hello." Julie, afraid she was being pitied, didn't raise her eyes. Never again would she be at ease with Dick—never after that awful conversation at the dance.

"You've been going around in a fog lately. What's the matter with you?"

Julie flushed. "Me? Nothing. I've been pretty busy at the farm." Her flush deepened because the reply sounded so lame.

"What's going on? Your dad sick?"

"No, but we've been raising that litter of puppies and all." She stopped short, biting her lip. Here she was talking about dogs again, just as she had at the Frolic.

"How many pups are there?"

"Three." Julie mumbled the answer.

"Three? That's not many. They must be getting pretty old now."

Six weeks, Julie wanted to say proudly. You ought to see them. They're butter balls, as sturdy as if Scarlet had nursed them herself. But she kept wondering if Dick were continuing the conversation just to be kind, and she felt sure that none of the other girls would spend time alone with Dick discussing a litter of pups. She couldn't think what they would discuss, but not puppies. In the end all she could do was nod her head.

"How old?" Dick seemed bound to pursue the subject.

"Six weeks—today."

"Think I'll stop by and have a look at 'em on my way home."

Julie glanced up guardedly but she couldn't keep the surprise out of her voice. "Today?"

"Sure, what's the matter with today?"

Julie shook her head. "Nothing's the matter," she said.

When they got down from the bus at the lane Julie noticed that Dick didn't offer to carry her books, yet she remembered having seen him lugging a stack of Connie Blake's books down School Road just the other afternoon. She hurried along the path, although the boy was inclined to loiter, kicking at stones, bending to pick up a stick, sniffing the good country smell. Julie didn't pause, as she usually did, at the turn where the valley spread below the road. She almost ran down the winding hill, and ended up breathless at the yard gate.

"Pups in the house?" asked Dick.

"No, they're in the pen now. Behind the barn." Julie took him out to them at once.

Dick leaned over the wire and picked up one of the balls of fluff that came bounding toward them. His wide mouth broke into a grin and his eyes crinkled at the corners. "Golly! Aren't they something!"

Julie, watching him, smiled, forgetting herself for the first time since Dick had joined her on the bus. "They're pretty sweet." She leaned across the fence and scooped up a wriggling body with one hand. "Look at this one."

Dick looked and nodded. "You got them all named?"

"Uh-uh. Just pet names, of course. This is Sonny. That's Cocoa you're holding, and the one in the pen is Sistie." As she spoke Julie reached over to rumple Sistie's bobbing head.

Dick put Cocoa down and took Sonny from Julie just as Tom Ferguson came around the barn, bound for the truck patch with a wheelbarrow load of manure. " 'Lo, Dick," he called. "You're a stranger 'round here."

Julie didn't look up. Why did Dad have to say that—as though they had missed Dick?

"Hello, Mr. Ferguson. Some pups you've got!"

Tom put down the barrow and walked over. "Daggone nuisance," he complained, nevertheless grinning. "Julie and I've been playing wet nurse. Hear about it?"

Dick shook his head.

Tom told the story while Julie crouched by the pen, letting the dogs bite at her fingers through the wire. She was glad, as her father talked, that she'd stuck to her part of the feeding bargain, though the night vigils had become increasingly hard. Their mutual concern for the pups had built a new sense of companionship between herself and her dad. It was the one good thing that had come out of the long weeks since the dance.

"The four-o'clock shifts were the worst," Tom was saying with a chuckle. "One night I slept right through the alarm, but Julie never missed. Not once!"

He's talking about me as though I'm a person, not a child, Julie noticed. There was a decided difference. But she noticed, too, that Dick wasn't really listening to what her father was saying. He was being polite, and replying, "Boy!" and, "Gee, I'll bet that was tough!" but his eyes were wandering and his feet were restless. It never occurred to Julie to wonder if perhaps he were bored with grown-up conversation and wished Mr. Ferguson would go on about his business. She only suspected he wanted to get on home. She stood up nervously, and fidgeted until her dad finished his recounting and went back to his barrow, calling over his shoulder, "Better give 'em fresh water, Julie," as he stooped for the handles.

Julie hesitated a minute, waiting for Dick to go, but the boy followed her to the tap in the barn while she rinsed the water bowl and filled it. Then, when courtesy certainly required nothing further, he walked back to the yard gate with her. She couldn't understand it; she felt uncomfortable and tongue-tied. "Well," she said abruptly, "goodbye."

A flicker of surprise crossed Dick's eyes but his face was expressionless. "S'long," he replied as the gate clicked shut. "Take care." He struck out across fields in the direction of the Webster farm, whistling. Julie walked straight into the house.

With the door shut behind her, Julie leaned against it and let out a long breath of relief. Now that Dick was gone she wondered, for a reckless instant, if he had come today in an effort to get back on their old, friendly footing. What wouldn't she give to have the days of last summer back—the long, lazy days when they had explored the creek together and had taken picnic lunches up to the tree house! She wondered what Dick would be doing this summer, after school closed. He won't be coming here, she told herself firmly. He just came today out of a sense of duty. He doesn't like *me* anymore.

Yet all the next day she felt lighter and happier, because Dick had come to see the dogs. It was Friday, a balmy day, glistening and mild. Julie always liked Fridays, because the next day would be Saturday and especially because art class came once a week on Friday afternoons. Most of the girls hated art. They disinterestedly tried to draw the assignments Miss Farrell gave out, then giggled over their terrible results, knowing in advance that they were destined to get merely average grades.

"Art," they grumbled each Friday noon. "Ugh!" And Julie was embarrassed to admit that she looked forward to art, that it was one of the shining spots in her week.

Privately she thought Miss Farrell, new to the faculty this year, was beautiful, with her curling brown hair and her sympathetic hazel eyes that were young enough to meet Julie's own without the weight of years between them. Even the *smell* of the art classroom delighted her. It was a smell of paints and paper and charcoal all mixed up. Just to walk through the door gave her a thrill of anticipation. She itched to get a crayon or paintbrush in her hand and a piece of clean drawing paper before her. At these moments she felt capable of great things.

Julie couldn't remember how long she had wanted to be an artist, but it was all bound up with her mother and that same smell of paper and paints. Dimly—very dimly—she could remember sitting in the bay window of the second-floor sewing room that Mother had made into a studio. She'd always sat cross-legged, her feet tucked under her, frowning with concentration as she tried to copy, with five-year-old fingers, the things her mother drew.

She remembered her gratification when Margaret Field had taught her to draw "distant trees" in contrast to "trees close to"; it was her first experience of perspective. She remembered, also, a fairy tale of Hans Christian Andersen's her mother had told. It was called *The Galoshes of Fortune*.

These galoshes had this peculiarity, that whoever put them on would immediately find himself in whatever time, place, and condition of life he wished for. Julie had known at once what she'd desire, and she had told her mother solemnly. "To be eighteen and to be able to paint like you!"

Now, years later, she still wanted the same thing. As far back as that half-remembered day Julie had said to herself: When I grow up I'm going to be an artist. But she had never said it aloud. Not yet. It was something so personal that she had to save it.

On this particular Friday the art teacher was late. Nobody minded but Julie, and she didn't show it. The girls all stood around, or sat on the tables, and yawned. When Miss Farrell finally arrived they made a great bustle of starting to work, then sat and chewed their pencils and wriggled, looking out of the windows with longing. It was such a beautiful day!

But Julie, sitting opposite Anne and Shirley, began to lose all sense of time. She finished the whole assignment and began to pencil little sketches on the margin of her paper. They were thumbnails of the puppies, jumping in the air, running, curled up asleep. She tried hard to capture their foolish high spirits.

Miss Farrell came up behind her. "You like to draw dogs, don't you?"

Julie nodded. "We have some collie pups. I'd like to make them look solid underneath the fluff and I'd like to make them look lively, too, but I can't seem to manage."

Miss Farrell laughed. She had a deep, throaty laugh that always made Julie feel keyed up and adventurous. "They're both difficult things to do," she said, "but these aren't bad tries, Julie. They have a lot of action."

They went on talking for a while, both forgetting the routine assignment. "Try sketching the puppies from life, rather than from memory," Miss Farrell advised. "Then bring the sketches to me. I'd like to see them." She patted Julie's shoulder encouragingly and walked on to the next pupil.

Julie sat very still. She kept looking down at her drawing board but she wondered if Anne and Shirley, sitting opposite, had heard. Timidly she glanced toward them, but they were engrossed in conversation, their heads bent over their work but their lips moving in rapid whispers.

". . . Sidney's party," Julie heard. "Yes, Dick Webster's taking Connie. Didn't you know?"

Julie's face was hidden behind her tilted board, but she could feel a hot flush climb from her neck to her cheeks. In an instant Miss Farrell's praise was forgotten. Only the words she had overheard jumped clear. Sidney was having a party and she, Julie, hadn't been invited. Dick was taking Connie. Yesterday hadn't meant a thing, then. She'd been right in the first place. Dick had been paying a duty call.

The flush receded and Julie's face froze to a blankness while she pretended to be engrossed in her drawing. The period dragged on to its end and she had to sit there, making meaningless lines on the paper while the last vestiges of her self-respect crumbled.

She hadn't been asked to Sidney's party. She was an outsider, a nobody—that's what she was! Julie punched the thumbtacks back into the spongy drawing board and scribbled her name on the upper right-hand corner of her assignment before handing it in. She wrote in backhand—Julie Ferguson—and stared down at the signature angrily. It was a stupid name.

"Coming, Julie?"

Anne was waiting in the doorway. They had their next class, algebra, together. "In a minute," Julie said.

Anne, to her relief, walked on. Julie followed slowly, making a deliberate effort not to catch up. She sat through the rest of the afternoon with her hands numb in her lap, her face expressionless, but her heart was pumping hotly and she was very wretched indeed. First she blamed herself; she was shy and plain—she deserved to be unpopular. Then she began making excuses. She lived too far out of town. Her clothes weren't as nice as the other girls'. Having no mother was an unfair handicap; there was no woman to tell her what to do.

The attack of self-pity lasted until she reached home. Then, safely beyond the clutching grasp of school things, she raced down the hill, changed like lightning into jeans, and ran to the pen to let out the puppies.

She took them down to the meadow beside the brook, and they romped about her in an ecstasy of joy at being released. Cocoa, entranced by a common white butterfly, tottered dizzily after it on his uncontrollable legs while Sistie set up a frantic yelping. Sonny, staying close to Julie, tangled with her feet, then emerged to somersault crazily over and over. Julie laughed at them and tried to forget the smart of her wounded pride. She sank down on the damp grass, and they swarmed around her, nipping at her fingers, swiping her face with caressing pink tongues. She lay down on her back, her eyes half-closed against the sun, and they scrambled across her stomach and tugged at her hair.

"Ouch!" she cried, sitting up. Surprised at her tone of voice, the pups stood off from her, panting. Then she gathered all three of them into the circle of her arms and held them, squirming, against her. They were so warm and cuddly. They loved her so blindly. "Babies," she whispered into their sweet-smelling fur.

She stayed in the meadow with them for a long time, lying on her stomach with her head propped in her hands while they made explorations near the brook. Sistie found a black bug and worried it, tossing it into the air and barking at it in abandoned excitement. Sonny watched her scornfully and trotted off toward the bridge on some important business, while Cocoa, exhausted from leaping for his butterfly, came back to Julie and started to chew the leg of her jeans.

Julie began to relax. She felt utterly spent of emotion. She could persuade herself, now, that she didn't care if Sidney had six parties and if Dick never spoke to her again in his life. School would be over soon, and she could spend all her time with the collies. She wouldn't ever have to leave the farm at all.

"Julie!" Tom Ferguson's bass voice rumbled down the slope.

Julie sat up and called, "I'm down here."

"Better bring the pups up. It's getting late."

A splash from the brook behind Julie interrupted her father's words. She whirled around to account for her charges, but only Sistie and Cocoa were in sight.

Alarmed, Julie ran toward the bridge. Before she reached the bank she could see Sonny's body thrashing in the shallow water. Fighting against the current, which had been quickened by spring rains, he looked like a blond rat, with his fur plastered against him.

Julie slid down the muddy bank on the seat of her jeans without stopping an instant. Wading into the stream without even kicking off her sneakers she fished Sonny out and held the puppy against her sweater.

"What happened, baby? You fall off the bridge?"

Sonny was shivering from fright and cold. He snuggled against her, burrowing with his head. Calling to the other pups and sheltering Sonny with her arm, Julie hurried up to the house.

Her father was waiting at the top of the rise.

"What happened?"

"Sonny fell into the stream. Must have lost his balance."

Tom held out his hands. "Give him to me. You put the other pups in the pen."

When Julie got to the house her father was rubbing Sonny down with an old bath towel. The pup was shivering visibly now, wobbling on his legs as the man roughed his fur up briskly.

Tom scowled at his daughter. "Get me a half teaspoon of whiskey," he said.

Julie helped her father to pour the whiskey down the dog's throat. Sonny choked and spluttered. Tom took him over to the stove and rolled him in a blanket, putting him in the packing box where the puppies had been raised.

"What were you doing when this pup fell off the bridge?" her father asked Julie.

Julie was ripping off her own wet shoes and socks. "Nothing."

Tom's voice grew sarcastic. "Nothing. That's obvious."

"I mean—I was right there. I just wasn't looking." It was a lame excuse.

"Do you realize, Julie, that there's ice water flowing in the brook this time of year?" Julie, rubbing her cold feet, nodded. "One bad chill can kill a six-week-old puppy." Tom snapped his fingers. "Kill him just like that." He looked at his daughter closely. "After all my work, five minutes' carelessness on your part . . ." He paused. "You've got to cut out the daydreaming, girl. I've told you that!"

Julie looked down at the wet shoes and socks on the floor. "All *my* work," her father had said. Not "our"— "*my*." He had forgotten the nights she had crawled out of bed to feed the puppies. He was talking to her like a child again, and all the sense of companionship that had been growing within her was lost. She felt suddenly resentful. An accident could happen to anybody!

But then she remembered that she had been daydreaming, as he called it—lying full length on the grass, only part of her thoughts on the pups. And if Sonny died it would be her fault. Hers. No one else's. Overwhelmed by responsibility too great to be borne, Julie suddenly swept up the shoes and socks and raced upstairs. Couldn't she ever do anything right—anything right at all? Would it always be like this—at home as well as at school? Would she always feel inferior and bungling?

Two little boys in corduroy pants were running sticks along the school-yard fence. "No more pencils; no more books," they chanted in a familiar rhythm.

One of the youngsters bent swiftly and picked up a stone, hurling it at the wheel of the school bus, and the driver leaned out the window and bawled at them, interrupting their singsong. They stuck out their tongues and were off down the shady street with a whoop, while Julie, waiting for the bus to start, seethed with the same impatience.

On her lap lay a drawing pad, wrapped and tied against prying eyes. Both hands held it tight, and her fingers curled around the edges. It was the only thing she was carrying home.

In the distance, loitering along, Julie could see Anne and Connie and Sue Downs. The sun spattered through the trees and fell on their bright cotton dresses. They'd be going to the drugstore, Julie knew, to have a milk shake in honor of the great event. School, at long last, was over.

The past month had been torture for Julie. She had been overcome by an attack of shyness out of proportion to her imagined hurts. Gradually she had felt her spirit folding up, layer after layer, until she couldn't see the people around her in proper focus at all. She kept out of the girls' way, feeling they didn't want her, instinctively trying to protect herself from possible snubs. Anne made a couple of overtures, but when Julie showed no response she gave up, turning to Connie. Life was too short to worry about Julie's moods.

Julie's discomfort reflected itself in her actions. She was either depressed and detached or she entered too determinedly into the conversation, laughing too loudly, saying things to cover her shyness that she thought might sound smart. But the girls just looked at her curiously, if they paid any attention at all.

When they discussed summer plans Julie felt especially left out. Anne was going to the seashore with her family. Sidney was going to camp, and so were Shirley and Sue. Connie Blake wasn't going anywhere. "I'm going to hold the home fort," she said when anybody asked her. "Wait'll you see the neat sunburn I can get right in our backyard!"

Julie wanted to say: "Ride out to the farm someday on your bike. There's a place in the brook Dick and I used to go swimming," but then she remembered about Dick and Connie and Sidney's party and she felt awkward.

It didn't matter anyway, she told herself. The June days at the farm were breathtakingly beautiful. She could get along without people. She had the pups.

Sonny, to Julie's enormous relief, had weathered the chill without ill effect. There had been a night and a day of anxiety, when Tom had watched over the puppy anxiously and Julie had crept about on tiptoe, as though she were in a sickroom, filled with guilt. Sonny had slept, curled in a ball, shivering slightly, but repeated doses of whiskey had warded off the pneumonia that both the girl and the man feared.

With Sonny's recovery her father's anger had cooled, but Julie still treated him cautiously, and kept, as much as possible, out of his way.

All three of the dogs now were getting to look more like collies and less like muffs. They were losing their stubby noses, the sable in their coats was darkening, and they had a leggy look that endeared them especially to Julie—why, she didn't know.

At Miss Farrell's suggestion, Julie had tried to sketch them, making an effort to catch the enthusiasm of their spirits, the tumbling awkwardness of their puppy antics, and transfer them to paper. Shyly she had shown a group of the sketches to Miss Farrell after school one afternoon. It had taken a good deal of watchful waiting, to catch the teacher completely alone.

But her patience was rewarded. "Why, Julie, these are splendid!" Miss Farrell said at once. "You can really draw!"

The words surrounded Julie and warmed her, making her eyes

44

shine. "They're nothing, really," she protested. "I can do better than that." But she was extremely proud of the sketches, and that night she hid them away in the bottom drawer of her bureau. Encouraged by the art teacher, she at once started to make plans for the summer, when she'd have all day to play with the puppies and learn to capture their moods.

She was eager to begin. As the bus bumped along, the sketch pad on her knees felt exciting just to touch, and the minute she reached home she intended to start some new drawings of the pups. What a wealth of work she'd have to show Miss Farrell in the fall!

But when she reached the farmhouse she discovered that Mrs. Mott had been laid up for a day. There were the beds to make, the dishes to be washed, and the vegetables for dinner to prepare. Her project with the puppies had to be put off.

The next morning, however, Julie raced through her housework and packed a picnic lunch. With her drawing equipment in the same basket as the sandwiches, she let the collies out of their pen and started up the brook.

They were ecstatic with joy at being with her. They would follow her anywhere now, and her whistle could call them in. They leaped about her, licking her hands with their salmon tongues, dancing off from her and returning with a rush, barking happily.

Julie walked up the brook for nearly half a mile. The border of trees which fringed the plowed fields changed to woodland, where the drying flowers of wild azalea and laurel fell in a flurry as Julie's shorts brushed the bushes.

The pups raced on ahead, exploring. "You don't know where I'm going," Julie told them. "You've never been there."

She came to a clearing at the brook's edge, a circular room in the woods. The sun fell clear and warm on the pine needles, but trees walled the place, making it shut and secret. "Here!" Julie said.

The dogs snooped about while she hung her basket from the dead limb of a pine tree. They seemed to understand that this was a room, and they must not venture into the surrounding woods.

A long branch, snapped off in a winter's storm, was flung on the ground in the clearing, and Julie dragged it off at once, tugging and pulling until she had it hidden in the woods. Aside from the branch, nothing was changed. There was the same pile of pink bricks, brought for the oven she had never built. There was the rusted grill. She was glad, now, that she hadn't told Dick Webster about this spot, as she had once meant to. She was glad it was entirely hers.

Julie spread her arms, half stretching, half embracing the friendly solitude. This is my place, she told the dogs silently. She was sure they understood because they seemed to want to stay there when she sat down.

She didn't take out her drawing things at once; she just lay on the pine needles, flat on her back, and soaked up the warmth of the sun. Contentment began to steal over her and she sighed deeply. This was good.

For a long time she lay there, her hands motionless on the pine needles. One by one the young collies joined her, stretching out singly on the ground, no longer a close huddle of bodies seeking one another's comfort but independent growing dogs.

Julie fell asleep, waking up when Sonny's tongue tickled her nose. She pulled the pup down on top of her, snuggling his lengthening head into her neck, then holding him off to gaze into his mournful almond eyes. Cocoa and Sistie, aroused by the soft shuffle, wriggled in between them, demanding their share of attention by biting at Julie's ears and playfully pulling her hair.

"Hey! Stop that!" But there was laughter in the girl's gasping voice, affection in the short slaps the dogs felt on their rumps. This was a game! They came back for more.

Tired at last and breathless, girl and dogs all gave up at once. The pups retired to stretch out again on the ground, and Julie, more from a feeling of duty than from ambition, took her sketch pad down from the hanging basket and leaned her back against a tree.

Then, without putting a mark on the paper, she sat and stared at the slow running water of the brook.

Her mind, behind her dreaming brown eyes, felt floating and free. Threads of thought crossed it, weaving and interweaving, so shimmery light that they scarcely left a pattern at all. She was in a picture gallery, and a group of people were standing before a painting on the wall. Julie couldn't see it, but she knew that it was hers. "Julie Ferguson's. One of the talented younger group." She smiled uncertainly.

Then everybody was dancing, and she was dancing with Dick and she floated, with never a thought of stumbling, or of hanging heavy on her partner's arm. Through the music she could hear Miss Farrell's grave, enthusiastic voice: "These are splendid, Julie. You can really draw." Then Julie knew what the painting on the walls of the gallery was. It was a picture of Scarlet, sable and white against the brush of green fields, standing with head high, her ruff wind-rippled, queenly, glorious.

"Julie Ferguson, the noted dog artist," Julie whispered aloud. Did famous artists, she wondered, draw especially dogs? Or would that be silly? She looked down at the blank piece of paper and yawned.

It was time, Julie decided, to eat her lunch. The puppies crowded around her, begging crusts from the thick sandwiches, teasing and rubbing their heads against her. Julie talked to them as she ate, scolding them. "Sistie, you're a big pig. That one was Cocoa's and you snatched it. Look at Sonny now. He doesn't act like that." Then she was afraid Sistie and Cocoa would guess that Sonny was her favorite and she gave them both an extra chunk of bread with a little meat inside.

Sonny sat on his haunches, watching Julie. At the special favor bestowed on his litter mates his ears flashed up in surprise. Julie tried to remember his expression of startled anger, but when she attempted to put it into a drawing it was too subtle for her pencil to portray.

She sketched for a while, lazily, and then started home. There was no hurry about anything. There would be other days. Long, drowsy summer days, undisturbed and uncomplicated by people. Except for her dad. And he was too busy with cultivating to bother about his daughter much.

She skirted the edge of the cornfield above the barn, guiding the dogs to one side so that they would not trample the tender green stalks. Peace enveloped her like a filmy scarf and she began to hum softly.

Then, simultaneously, she saw two things—Dick Webster, in overalls, at work in the barnyard, and the long lines of the familiar Lonsdale car. She stopped at the edge of the field and looked down, whistling the pups to her when they raced on ahead. Then, deliberately, she started toward the house.

Dick stopped work as she passed the barnyard gate and called out to her, "Hi, Julie."

"Hi," Julie said. She knew he expected her to be surprised to see him there, knew he thought she would stop and question him, but she walked right on. Mr. Lonsdale and her father were bringing two grown dogs on leashes up the path toward the kennel.

"There she is now," she could hear her dad say.

Philip Lonsdale handed the leash he held to the other man and hastened toward Julie and the pups, bending down to scoop Cocoa into his arms when he was the first to reach him. He held him for an instant, hand under the collie's chin, then set him down with a low whistle and turned to Sistie.

Ferguson stood by without speaking, a smile curving the corners of his mouth. His glance flashed momentarily to his daughter, but Julie was looking at the pups. The breeder crouched in the path to run his hands over Sonny, then looked up in pleased surprise.

"We've got something here," he said.

Ferguson nodded, grinning. "I've been thinking so, too."

Mr. Lonsdale rose, and Julie could hear one of his knees crackle. "Unless I miss my guess, they'll each be as fine a dog as Scarlet. Or maybe finer. Who knows?"

Finer than Scarlet? Julie, looking at the gawky youngsters, couldn't believe that they could grow to such perfection. Her expression showed it, and Mr. Lonsdale laughed.

"Don't believe it, eh, Julie?"

Julie didn't meet his eyes. "Scarlet was—beautiful."

But the men didn't wait for her reply. Mr. Lonsdale was slapping the farmer affectionately on the back. "You're to be congratulated, Tom," he said. "Not another man I know could have pulled those pups through."

Tom was always fair. "You've Julie to thank as much as me," he said. "She spelled me with the night feedings."

"Julie, my dear, I do thank you," said Mr. Lonsdale, gravely. He bowed to her, every inch the gentleman, but Julie still didn't raise her eyes.

"That's all right," she muttered, ashamed, as she said the words, that she couldn't be as gracious as he.

The men walked on toward the barn and Julie followed them to put her charges into the puppy pen. Sistie and Sonny and Cocoa raced on ahead, wildly curious about the two dogs Ferguson had on the leash, yet almost equally intrigued by the pair of strange trouser legs. They sniffed and barked, eyes alert, tails wagging like fast-set metronomes. Mr. Lonsdale turned at the barn door and watched them, his hands dragging down the pockets of his gray plaid sport coat, and a smile of satisfaction spreading across his thin face.

"There's a spirit to a dog that grows up with a child that you don't get in a kennel-bred dog," he said.

Dick, emerging from the black interior of the barn with a pitchfork in his hand, heard the remark and couldn't keep a twinkle from his eye as he glanced toward Julie. Tom stopped the boy and introduced him to Mr. Lonsdale.

"Dick Webster. He's going to help me out a bit this summer," Julie heard him say.

Her premonition was confirmed into fact. Dick would be at the farm every day! She ducked around the wall toward the puppy pen as Dick replied in a voice that was strong and easy, "Afternoon, sir."

Sistie and Sonny were inside the wire, but Cocoa, the rascal of the three, had spied a chicken and was leaping after it merrily, deaf to Julie's calls.

"Cocoa! Come here! Cocoa. Come here this minute." Julie's voice was angry and insistent, and as she moved forward in pursuit she felt Dick's pitchfork gently prod her back.

"Be calm, child!" he teased her, but she didn't look back.

Finally all three of the pups were in the pen, fed and watered. Julie went to the house, rounding the yard and going in the back way, because her father and the breeder sat on the two round-backed wooden chairs on the stoop. The windows were open, and she could hear snatches of their conversation as she washed up and combed bits of leaf and stick out of her hair.

"I'd like to leave the pups out here for the summer," the dog breeder was saying, and Julie's comb paused while she began to think of just what that would mean—two more dogs to feed and water all summer long.

Then, with a shock, she realized they weren't talking about the new boarders. They were talking about her puppies—Sistie and Cocoa and Sonny—because her father was saying: "Let's see. They'll be six months old by the end of September."

Julie's hand with the comb came down to her lap, and she stared unseeing into the mirror.

"That'll give them a good start," she heard Mr. Lonsdale add. "I'll keep the pick and sell the others, I guess."

Julie ran to the window and closed it with a bang that shook the old house.

"Hey, Julie, careful up there!" she heard her father boom.

But she wouldn't listen. She wouldn't! They were her dogs. She'd nursed them. She'd raised them. She wouldn't face the fact that Mr. Lonsdale could just, cold-bloodedly, take them away. Then she became a bit more calm. September was a long time off. Anything could happen by then. Maybe they wouldn't find buyers, her dad and Mr. Lonsdale. Or maybe, even if two of the pups were sold, the pick of the litter would be left with them over the winter. Surely that would be it. Sonny would stay on. And the following spring was too far distant for Julie's mind to make real—endless, countless months and weeks and days in a future that had no substance, that might never even come.

Then, once again her calmness deserted her and a fury began to build up within her until her chest felt tight and her heart pounded. She sat on the edge of the old spool bed that had been her grandmother's and let her feet dangle free of the floor. She could hear Dick's whistle as he cut across the meadow toward home. She could hear the smooth starting of the Lonsdale car. She could hear her father close the front door and tramp through the hall to the shed.

Her teeth locked tight, she went downstairs and filled the teakettle with water. She lighted the gas under the peeled potatoes, and, taking the bread knife from its rack, walked over to the battered tin bread box. Tom, rubbing his dripping face with a towel, came through the kitchen door, and suddenly, clutching the bread in its plastic wrapper, Julie whirled on him.

"Why did you have to hire Dick Webster?" she cried. "Who do you think I am? Don't I have any rights around here?"

The bread knife clattered to the floor, and as her father was still lowering the towel from his face she brushed past him and fled up the stairs, slamming her bedroom door.

The man below stood still in the doorway and looked after her with a baffled frown. Funny, he was thinking, I was sure she liked that kid.

Out in their pen, spotting an intruding rabbit, the collies began to yelp.

In the rural-delivery box by the main road was a cardboard carton with a B. Dalton label addressed to Miss Julie Ferguson.

Julie, collecting the mail, plumped right down in the coarse field grass and tore at the flap with impatient fingers. Two books were inside. One, with a painting of a collie's head on its jacket, was called *Lassie Come Home*. The other was a book of short stories about dogs illustrated by little line drawings. On its flyleaf was a message in an angular, masculine hand:

For Julie
with my deep appreciation
Philip Lonsdale

Appreciation for what, Julie wondered momentarily. Oh, of course! For helping dad with the pups. Julie ran her hand over the jackets appreciatively. They were slick and crisp. The books had a clean, new smell about them, too, so different from the books Julie borrowed occasionally from the Meadowbrook Public Library that she brought them close to her nose and sniffed at them with lively pleasure.

How nice of Mr. Lonsdale!

"Nice!" She said the word aloud and began to examine the illustrations in the book of short stories more carefully, comparing them with her own sketches of the pups. That they were more mature she could see, but she thought they lacked action sometimes, and animation, perhaps because this artist had never been blessed with such models as hers! She grinned at her own imagination, and held the books to her as

52

she hurried down the lane toward home. As far back as she could remember, nobody had ever given her a book before.

There weren't many books at the farm. Dad had a couple beside the clock on the kitchen shelf. They were forbidding, dark green volumes on animal husbandry and soil conservation. Mother's art books were packed away in the attic where there was also a dusty collection of novels and popular histories, now years out of date. But of new books there were none, until these two. Julie began to wish she had a bookcase.

Wanting to show her gift to someone, she carried the books into the shed where Mrs. Mott was doing the laundry, up to her elbows in soapsuds over an old-fashioned metal washtub.

"Mrs. Mott, look! I got a present."

Mrs. Mott was as flat as her washboard, with faded hair drawn tight back over a narrow band. Her eyes were faded too, a watery blue, with purple half-moons under them. But she straightened up and looked at Julie kindly.

"Books!" Julie said, holding them out.

"Books, eh?" Mrs. Mott's kindliness turned to suspicion. "Who's sending you books?"

"Mr. Philip Lonsdale," Julie told her proudly.

Mrs. Mott returned to her suds with shaking head. She didn't have much use for books. It was her private opinion that Julie fiddle-faddled away too much time as it was, at an age when a girl should be learning to sew and housekeep.

"What's the matter, Mrs. Mott?"

"Y' get notions out of books, notions out of your place in life," the woman sniffed.

Julie wandered away, feeling deflated. She thought of going to find her father, but he was tilling late corn in the south field, and she'd noticed that even at breakfast his eyes seemed sunk in his head from weariness. She doubted if he'd be much interested in the books, either. Dick she had been avoiding ever since he had come to work on the farm. When she did run across his path he was apt to ignore her, steeped in his own busyness, proud that he was doing a man's work. At other times, less self-important, he would make overtures, but Julie kept linking him in her mind with Connie Blake, and she felt clumsy and unattractive. Nine times out of ten she answered him shortly and hurried away as soon as she could.

Today, however, she met Dick on the path to the barn, and she couldn't resist showing him the books.

"Yeah," he said, wiping his hands on his pants before he took the books from her. "Swell. Loan 'em to me after you've finished?"

"Sure," said Julie, flattered. "In a couple of days. I read fast."

It was her regular morning job to exercise the boarding dogs. She parked the books on the barnyard wall while she ran first the older dogs, then the pups. Finally she was free to go up to her secret room beside the brook.

She took Sonny with her, reluctantly leaving the other pups behind because all three of them together were too much to handle. They were apt to go berserk from sheer youthful exuberance and run wild in the planted fields.

Sonny was the most manageable of the three. With every added week of life he grew in both stature and personality. His almond eyes became bright with understanding when Julie issued familiar commands, and he wriggled with self-consciousness when she praised him.

When she let him out of the pen this morning he was ecstatic with delight, and canine hero worship was evident in the excited prancing of his forelegs and the wagging of his plumed tail. He knew the way up the brook by heart and he led Julie there, dropping down by her side on the pine needles when she sprawled out with her book.

For a long time there was silence under the arching trees. Sonny fell asleep, then, awakening, got up and stretched fore and aft, collie-fashion. For a moment he stood uncertainly, looking toward the brook, then began to wash Julie's face with his warm tongue.

Julie, absorbed, pulled him down against her, one brown arm around his ruff. The outer coat felt harsh to her fingers but the inner coat was soft and furry and very thick. Sonny tumbled, and together the dog and girl rolled over, laughing.

They wrestled awhile, then fell quiet, and Julie held Sonny's head between her lean young hands, smoothing back the ruff. She looked into his eyes very seriously and talked to him, spacing her words deliberately in an effort to make him understand.

"You're my dog," she told him. "You're my dog just the way Lassie was Ronny's dog. If they take you away, you'll come back to me, won't you? Won't you?" she cried.

Sonny looked at her pleadingly, trying to comprehend. He laid his muzzle against her cheek and held it there, telling her he adored her. Nevertheless, two tears trickled out of the corners of Julie's eyes and slid down to drop with tickling coldness into the lobes of her ears. She could not convince herself that, no matter how strong his urge, Sonny could ever come home as Lassie had from the far north of Scotland to the little village in Yorkshire where his young master lived. Sonny could never swim rivers and cross mountains and skirt cities to get back. Only the mythical Lassie could do that.

Yet the sentiment and the heartbreak of Eric Knight's great collie story swept over her. She herself was Lassie, daring all, suffering all with an undying loyalty, trying to get back to her master. But Sonny and Lassie were really one. The dream merged and melted. She jerked her mind back to reality and sat up, head in hands.

Maybe, she began to think—searching for some escape from the fear that Sonny would be taken from her—maybe it will be this dog that Mr. Lonsdale will choose to keep. And if it *is* Sonny, maybe he'll be allowed to stay on here at the farm for a long time. Her head nodded, postponing the evil day.

But it wasn't a really satisfactory solution. It was too temporary, and it lacked her father's approval, because when she approached him that evening and said, hopefully, "D'you suppose, Dad, when Mr. Lonsdale takes his pick of the litter, he may leave that pup with us over the winter?"

He grunted without conviction. "Maybe," he said.

The "maybe," for Julie, was "no." She left her father sitting on the stoop, leaning back in his chair with an expression of exhaustion, and walked out to the pen. She put her hand through the wire and let the pups lick it and nibble at her fingers. Her eyes were big and very dark.

Tom Ferguson watched her as she walked slowly back. She would have passed him and gone on into the house, but he called to her.

"Julie."

Julie, reaching for the handle of the screen door, turned.

"Where've you been all day?"

"Up the brook."

"Alone?"

"With Sonny."

Tom frowned. "Did you get the truck patch weeded?"

The arrival of the books had put the weeding job entirely out of Julie's mind. "I'll do it tomorrow," she said.

Her father's scowl deepened, but he didn't speak. Julie went on into the house.

The next day she got at the weeding early, before the sun was hot, and by noon the worst of the job was behind her. Tom, backing the Ford out of the barn to go on a quick errand to town, called to her. "Want to come along?"

He waited while Julie washed her hands, then raced the old car up the hill and out to the road. The air felt cool on Julie's face, and she had a comforting sense of accomplishment. "The weeding's almost done," she said.

"I saw it was. Good job."

Outside the drugstore, where Tom parked the car to go to the hardware store opposite, Julie met Connie Blake. Connie was nibbling at an ice-cream cone, and she sauntered over to the car to talk. "Hi, Julie. Hot, isn't it?"

Julie nodded, wishing she had taken time to comb her hair. "I'll say." Here was her opportunity. Now she should suggest, "How about coming out to the farm this afternoon for a swim?" Just the sight of Connie made her realize how lonely she'd been for another girl to talk to. But somehow the invitation didn't get past her lips.

Connie licked a dribble of ice cream up the side of the cone. "What's new?"

Julie shrugged. "Nothing. It's been a dumb summer." It hadn't. It had been a beautiful summer with the dogs at the farm. There had been long, lazy days so lovely that they had become part of Julie's consciousness, tangled and twining together. But there had been no conventional excitement. To Connie it might have seemed dumb.

Connie raised her eyebrows. "You can swim out there, can't you?"

Julie nodded. "Oh, sure. You know, I was thinking—"

But just then her dad came up. "'Lo, Connie," he said, lifting a burlap bag into the back of the car.

"Hello, Mr. Ferguson," Connie's smile was friendly. "I guess you're busy out at the farm."

"Busy's the word." Tom grinned back at her. "Why don't you run out and see us one of these days?"

Julie wriggled in her seat. Now why did Dad have to say that? It made it look as though she needed company. Well, she did, but she didn't want Connie Blake to know.

"I'd like to," Connie said.

Tom climbed behind the wheel. "Drive you out now, 'f you want to come. Julie'll take you for a swim. Tell you what. Dick's been working pretty hard this week. I'll let him off and he can go along, too."

Julie's hands were clenched and the smile was frozen on her face. She wished her father would shut up—shut up—shut up!

"Dick? Dick Webster?"

"Uh-huh." Tom was leaning across Julie to open the door. He was no man to waste time on decisions. "Coming?"

Connie hesitated. "I'd like to! But how would I get back? And I don't have my suit."

Julie tried to nudge her father, tried to make him see he shouldn't urge her, but he was oblivious.

"I'll drive you to the crossroads for the five-o'clock bus, and Julie's got an old suit around somewhere. Haven't you, Julie?" He was making everything pointedly easy, and Julie couldn't understand why.

"An *awfully* old one," she said, making the suit sound impossible.

But Connie said with a laugh: "Swell. I'd love to come."

They waited while she called her mother from the drugstore. Julie sat silent in the car, but Tom drew on his pipe as though he was pleased with himself. "Do you good to have some young folks around once in a while," he said. "You've been spending too daggone much time up the brook."

All the way out to the farm Julie wondered whether Connie would have come if Dick Webster hadn't been mentioned. She sat in moody thought while Connie and her father chatted across her. Connie had a way with older men as well as with younger ones. She questioned

Tom about the stock and the crops and listened to his rambling answers as though she were really interested.

When they rounded the turn above the valley she broke off in the middle of a sentence and caught her breath. "It's beautiful out here!" she said. "Does your farm have a name?"

Julie's eyes suddenly glowed. "Deepdale," she said although her father shook his head.

Tom looked at Julie in surprise. "Huh?"

"Deepdale," Julie repeated softly, cherishing the word. "I found it on the old deed in that tin box in the attic."

"It's the perfect name," said Connie, and Julie flashed her a look of appreciation.

"I think so, too."

Tom let the girls out at the yard gate, and Julie took Connie up to her bedroom while she went on to the attic to hunt up the faded blue bathing suit she had discarded the year before. When she came back to the bedroom she found Connie turning the pages of the book of dog stories.

"These are neat," Connie said.

Julie nodded. "Mr. Lonsdale sent them to me," she said proudly.

"I'd like to read them sometime."

"I'll lend them to you," offered Julie at once, then remembered, "After Dick. I promised them to him first."

Connie put the book back on the windowsill with the other. "Some-day," she said dreamily, "I'm going to write a book. Or work for a publishing house. Aunt Helen works for a publishing house in Philadelphia, you know." She ducked her head suddenly and peered at the backbone of the book of dog stories. "*This* publishing house!" she cried, pleased.

Julie took the book from the sill and examined the name with interest. "Really? What does she do?"

"She's secretary to the art director," Connie replied promptly. "It sounds like a wonderful job. Artists from all over bring their drawings in and Aunt Helen gets a chance to meet lots of them. The artists, I mean."

"Maybe she even met the artist who did this book."

"Maybe," said Connie. "I wouldn't be surprised."

"You know," said Julie without meaning to, "I've been making some drawings of the puppies this summer. Just for fun." She was aching to show someone her sketches, yet she didn't know what had possessed her to tell Connie Blake.

But Connie sounded impressed. "You have? Can I see them?"

Julie backtracked fast. "They're nothing much. You wouldn't be interested."

"Oh, but I would!" Connie insisted. "Please let me."

So Julie brought the sketches from the bottom bureau drawer and sat down on the bed beside Connie, turning them over one by one.

"They're wonderful!" Connie praised. "Why, Julie, I never knew you could draw like this."

Julie flushed with pleasure. "I'm not really very good."

"But you are! I think your drawings are every bit as good as lots I've seen in books. Every bit."

The praise was like music. Julie warmed to Connie by the moment. When Dick's voice, from the yard gate, yelled to them to hurry if they were going swimming, she insisted that Connie wear her good suit.

In the old blue suit, faded and threadbare, Julie knew she looked a sight. But when Connie, on the way to the dam, told Dick about the sketches and said, "They're marvelous, really!" the compliment made up for her self-consciousness.

Swimming at the dam was fun. Overhanging branches kept the brook water cool. Though the pool was small, it was deep, and there was a rough diving board with a good spring to it. They played water tag, and Julie was faster than Connie and almost as fast as Dick. Buoyed by an inner excitement, she laughed more than usual and never once wondered whether Dick might not be paying slightly more attention to the visitor than to her.

On the way home Julie showed Connie the pups. "Sonny's my pet!" she explained. "You can talk to Sonny. He knows what you're saying."

Connie liked Cocoa. "He's the rascal of the bunch," Julie told her. "He's always getting into trouble with Dad."

Sistie was now the smallest of the litter, dainty and feminine, but as she had grown older she had developed a slight droop to her left ear that Tom feared would spoil her chances as a show dog. Julie didn't tell Connie about the droop. She was always especially nice to Sistie because of it.

Tom was in high spirits when he drove Connie to the bus. "That's what you need," he told Julie when he came back. "More companionship." Julie made no comment but her animation lasted all through the evening, and when she went to bed she lay for a long time staring happily into the darkness.

Connie thought her drawings were good!

Connie went to visit Anne at the shore and didn't get back to the farm, but Julie scarcely noticed. She was spending every spare moment with her sketch pad in front of her, making dozens of new drawings of the dogs.

Evenings, she read her mother's art books, rooted out of the attic and dusted. Most of them were far beyond her, but here and there she picked up an idea which she earnestly tried to interpret as she drew. To her father she seemed forgetful and absent-minded, but Julie's hidden life was wildly exciting. She was afire with ambition, for she had a wonderful, even alarming—but as yet unspoken—idea.

For weeks now Julie had known that she *must* keep Sonny. Somehow, by hook or by crook, she was determined to discover a way. At first she felt as though she were in a closed room with no opening, no escape. But gradually the idea took possession of her, and though it frightened her so that her throat ached and her stomach muscles clenched, it grew and grew.

Its seed was in a remark of Connie's. She had said, "I think your drawings are every bit as good as some I've seen in books," and Julie had cherished the praise and returned to it again and again. Suppose Connie were right! Suppose, just possibly, somebody might buy the drawings—pay money for them—enough money so that Julie could in turn buy Sonny for her very own!

At first the idea was just another daydream, but gradually it began to take the shape of reality. Julie was ready to seize on any possibility that would allow her to keep the collie. The thought of separation was too much to be borne.

From the imprint on the jacket, Julie copied the name of the publisher of Mr. Lonsdale's gift book of dog stories, and one night when her dad had to drive to Meadowbrook for supplies, she rode along. There was a Philadelphia telephone directory in the drugstore booth. She could look up the address there.

That night she came close to confiding her wildly courageous scheme to her father. She needed to tell someone, and she wanted to tell him, but he was in one of his unapproachable moods, distant and silent.

"Dad," she began tentatively, "you know those books Mr. Lonsdale gave me—"

Tom, driving along at his usual breakneck speed, merely grunted.

"Remember the one with the sketches of dogs in it?"

"Sketches?" Dogs?" Tom frowned.

Julie nodded eagerly. "Yes. You remember! You laughed at one where a dachshund—"

Tom swerved suddenly to avoid a car that plunged unexpectedly out of a side road directly into his path on the highway. His frown deepened. "Look, Julie, tell me sometime again, will you? I'm—" he hesitated. "I've just got a lot of things on my mind."

Julie knew what the things were. A calf was sick; the tractor had broken down; there was a leak in the roof of the sheep pen. She quieted obediently, consoling herself with the thought that the chances were her dad would only laugh at the scheme anyway. It *was* a wild idea.

But that night, late, she tucked a slip of paper under the stacks of clean handkerchiefs in her bureau drawer. On it was a publisher's address, but there was really no need to save it. Julie knew the street number by heart.

She had been to Philadelphia often, because the city was a scant half hour from Meadowbrook by train. She had been with her class to tour Independence Hall and other historic buildings. She had been in two or three times with Mrs. Sawyer and Anne. She had driven in with her dad when he went on occasional business. But she had never been to the city alone, and just to contemplate such a venture made her spine tingle with fear.

Yet if she had to—and she did have to!—she could find her way to the publishing house and to Connie's Aunt Helen. Artists from all over brought their drawings in. Connie had said so.

Of course, Julie knew, she was terribly young. She wasn't a proper artist. But just last month she had read a newspaper account of a book written by a girl of seventeen. Maybe a teenage artist could be successful, too. Anyway, it was the only possible chance to secure Sonny. She had to take it.

Alone, she went to work. She picked blueberries and sold them, earning enough money for a box of soft colored pencils. These she used instead of the black drawing pencil to which she was accustomed.

For a long time her results failed to satisfy her, but gradually she became more skilled at the new technique. She watched the collies closely, spending all her free time with them. She sketched, tore up the drawings, and started again. Of her early summer work she selected a few of the better drawings, but the collection looked pitifully small.

As August sped toward September and the opening of school grew nearer, Julie's determination increased. She felt completely detached from everything except her drawing. She avoided Dick automatically, just as she avoided trying to imagine what it would be like to be a sophomore. She had room in her heart and mind only for Sonny and for her sketching. She spent more and more time in her place up the brook.

One afternoon Dick surprised her there. He crashed unexpectedly through the underbrush into the clearing and Julie sprang to her feet and hid her drawing pad behind her back.

"You followed me!" Julie accused him, angry that he had violated her privacy.

"Nope." Dick shook his head. "Just followed the path you've worn." Then he saw that her hands were behind her back. He grinned like a mischievous small boy. "Ha! Secrets!"

Julie reddened beneath her freckles. Her chin snapped up and she was on the defensive at once. "So what?"

Dick raised an eyebrow dramatically and his eyes twinkled. "So you're going to have to let me see."

"I won't."

"You will!" The boy teased the girl, their words following a time-worn pattern both had outgrown. Dick took a step forward, and, obeying a primitive instinct, Julie turned and ran.

Other summers, she could have beaten Dick, given a start. But the long days of inactivity told. This year she was soft. Before she had raced two hundred yards up the brook's slippery bank her heart was pounding and her breath was coming in gasps. Only Sonny, bounding along behind her, seemed to be enjoying the game.

Knowing she would be caught, Julie whirled and faced the laughing boy. "Dick Webster, don't you dare!" she cried as he came on toward her. There was no playfulness in her voice now. It was tense and furious.

Neither of them saw Sonny's ears prick up, but as Dick leaped a dead log to reach his quarry, a flash of gold and white hurtled through the air and Julie caught a glimpse of the collie's curving eyetooth as his lips curled back in a snarl.

"Sonny!"

Julie's voice stopped the dog a fraction of a second before the pointed teeth would have buried themselves in Dick's shoulder. As it was, only the boy's shirt tore downward with a ripping sound as Sonny dropped obediently to the earth. The forty-pound pup looked at his mistress apologetically, wagging his tail. How was a dog to know? It had looked like a romp, but then—

Julie looked anxiously at Dick's torn shirt. "Did he hurt you?"

Dick felt his shoulder. "Nope. But he sure would have. What d'you think of that!"

All the fight in Julie dissolved. Unexpectedly she held out the sketch pad. "Here. You can see it if you want. I was just making a drawing of Sonny, that's all."

Dick looked at her, standing there defenseless. "Never mind. I was only trying to get your goat," he muttered.

The pup had crossed to Julie and was rubbing against her jeans. Julie ran her fingers down his head and entangled them in his thickening ruff. Then impulsively she crouched and crushed the dog against her, still weak with wonder that he had leaped to her defense.

Dick stood above them, embarrassed. "You think a lot of that mutt, don't you?" he asked.

Julie nodded, wordless.

"I wouldn't let it get you, Ju." Dick's voice, almost tender, deliberately hardened with his next words. "There's no use pinin' for something that's not yours and never can be."

Fiercely Julie told him, "Sonny's going to be mine!"

She didn't see Dick's forehead wrinkle, but she felt his hard hands under her elbows as he pulled her to her feet. "Look, Julie," he said, gruffly, "you're getting yourself all tied up in knots. You used to be a good kid. Remember the fun we had, summers? Why can't you relax?"

The grip of Dick's hands went through Julie like an electric shock. She tore away from him. "I'm all right."

Dick shrugged. "Have it your way." He turned and started back toward the farm.

Julie waited until Dick's footsteps died away, then followed with Sonny. Outside the barn she hesitated, hearing voices. Her father was talking. "Yep," she heard him say, apparently answering some remark of Dick's. "Yep. A good thing school's starting in a couple of weeks. She's getting that attached to the pup, it'll almost kill her to have him taken away."

When school did start, in early September, Julie was present in flesh only. Her spirit was still at the farm with Sonny. It was easier that way. The gossip of the girls, the divided interest of the boys between football and feminine charms, swirled around her but scarcely touched her. She was filled with one increasing purpose.

A few days after the start of classes Julie took her sketches to the art teacher, and, without admitting her intention, asked for criticism. Miss Farrell turned the drawings over with interest, pleased to have such an ambitious pupil. "There's some fine work here. They show remarkable progress," she said.

Julie sighed aloud in relief. "You really think so?"

"I certainly do."

Julie plunged. "D'you think they're as good as dog drawings you've seen in books? I mean *some* books?"

The girl's heart-shaped face, upturned and earnest, appealed to the teacher. She seemed to yearn for praise and need it. Miss Farrell hesitated only an instant. "I—yes, I think they are—*some* books," she said.

Julie didn't smile. Her brown eyes were still wide and serious. But a glow swept over her, and as she gathered up the drawings and walked away she felt weightless, as though her feet scarcely touched the worn boards of the art classroom floor.

A week later Julie laid a definite plan. She intended to do something that shocked her strict sense of honor. She intended to play hooky from school.

Lying came unnaturally to Julie, and the arrangements she had to make seemed like a real network of deceit. She planned to leave school at noon, and she knew she would have to submit a note the next day to explain her absence. She had to have money for her carfare to the city and back, yet she couldn't explain to her father why she needed extra cash. She finally saved it by going without lunches for several days, and sat through afternoon classes with hunger gnawing at her empty stomach and fear crowding her chest.

The day she chose to go to town was a Wednesday. On Tuesday night she washed her hair and otherwise prepared herself for the interview as she would have primped for a party. She decided to wear her brown jacket and skirt instead of jeans, which seemed too informal to wear to a publisher's office, though Julie had little idea of what a publisher's office might be like.

After she got into bed the thought belatedly occurred to her that perhaps the art director would not be in, that perhaps the proper procedure would be to call for an appointment. She almost lost her courage then, and her forehead felt cold with sweat.

She slept fitfully. In the morning she awoke feeling beaten, as though a hundred rubber hammers had pounded at her flesh during the night. She dressed in an agony of apprehension, and gathered the ability to down a soft-boiled egg with her milk and toast only because her father might notice if she failed to eat.

The drawings, chosen from the dozens that Julie had made over the summer, were mostly those done in colored crayon. They looked, to her, so much more impressive than the earlier sketches in black pencil, of which she had included only a few. In the attic, weeks before, she had found an ancient portfolio of her mother's, a big cardboard affair, covered with blotchy paper and tied with tape gray with age. She packed her drawings in this because it looked professional, and because the scrawled name, Margaret Field, gave her a feeling that her mother was with her.

When she left for the bus with the huge portfolio tucked awkwardly under one arm, her father had long since gone to the fields, so she climbed the hill unnoticed and got the first lap of her adventure safely behind her.

On the bus she encountered Dick. "What you got there?" he asked immediately.

"Just some old drawings of Mother's Miss Farrell wanted to see," Julie answered, to quench his curiosity. She had been prepared to tell a fib, if she had to, but the experience was new to her, and she could feel a slow flush of shame creep up her neck.

At school she hid the portfolio in her gym locker, wedging it in catty-cornered and keeping the key in her jacket pocket. Every once in a while, as she sat through one endless class after another, she felt for it, to be sure it was safe.

As the morning dragged, the weight in Julie's chest grew. She sat in a daze of weakness and fear, and she never even heard her name when Mr. Blodgett, who taught Latin, called upon her to recite.

"I wonder if Julie Ferguson could return to the immediate present to consider the lost past?" the bespectacled teacher asked jokingly. A giggle ran through the classroom, and Julie, her eyes wide and vague, just caught the repeated and emphasized name.

"I don't know," she mumbled.

"You don't know what? You mean you don't know what I'm talking about?"

Julie looked down, beet red, and didn't answer.

"Is that it?" Mr. Blodgett pursued.

"I—I'm sorry. I wasn't listening."

Finally the five-minute bell, heralding the end of class, rang. Now that the moment was almost upon her when she must get the portfolio and walk out of the building to catch the 12:38 to town, Julie's knees turned to water and a trembling started in her thighs.

All the way to the station Julie fought a wild desire to bolt. Her mouth was dry and her knees would scarcely support her. She thought she'd feel better if only she could sit down.

As a matter of fact, once she felt the firm train seat beneath her, she did feel better. By a tremendous effort of will, there were even about ten minutes when she felt positively important. She was an artist, grown-up, going to Philadelphia with a portfolio of drawings. But then something in the way the conductor smiled down at her as he took her ticket made terror engulf her afresh. She wasn't grown-up; she was a very young girl. The other was make-believe.

Suburban towns flashed by while Julie made herself small and pushed closer to the window. Backyards passed, strung before Julie's eyes like played dominoes. She tried to watch everything closely, to keep from feeling sick.

Grass and trees gave way to smoke-smudged row houses, and Julie practiced repeating to herself the little speech with which she was prepared to greet the art director. "Good afternoon, Miss So-and-So." She must be very sure to ask Connie's Aunt Helen carefully about the name. "I've been wondering if you ever have any use . . ." No, that was terrible.

"I have some sketches I'd like to show you, in the hope that you might have use for something of this kind in one of your books." Certainly she hadn't got involved in such a long sentence when she composed the speech. How had it gone? How *had* it gone?

"Would you be willing to look at some dog drawings? I just thought maybe . . ." Each version sounded worse than the previous one, and the panic rising in Julie's chest was large in her eyes. "Would you have any use . . ." She tried again, but the wheels of the train haunted her. *Would you have any use, would you have any use, would you have any use* . . . The rhythm beat into her brain.

Julie jumped in alarm as the conductor announced her stop. With a stream of passengers she climbed from underground to the glistening station. People scurried to exits, but Julie stood undecided, not sure which way to turn. A man in a uniform was coming toward her. He had white hair and looked kind. Julie approached him timidly to ask directions.

"Walk straight across Fifteenth Street to Locust," he said.

"And could you tell me how to get to Fifteenth Street?" Julie persisted, although he looked too busy to be disturbed. The man looked at her over a pair of cloudy eyeglasses. "Go right out there, young lady, and follow the signs."

"Thank you very much." Julie scurried off, the big portfolio cutting into her underarm as she walked. After the airy cleanliness of the farm, the city streets were appallingly littered and dusty. While she waited for a light to change on Market Street she got something in her eye. It felt like an Indian arrowhead, although it was doubtless a speck of dust. Her eyes watered and reddened as she struggled fruitlessly to get it out.

After Market came Chestnut Street, then Walnut, and finally Locust. The address so carefully memorized was right on the corner. Julie suddenly found herself in the lobby of a tall office building, with a bank of elevators facing her across a slippery floor. The dust was still in her eye and seemed likely to remain there, but she couldn't give up now!

Finding the publisher's name and floor on a wall directory was easy, but gathering the courage to walk into one of the elevators was very difficult indeed. A distracted businessman with graying hair and two women engaged in conversation were Julie's only companions. The man got off at the third floor, and the young women at the fourth. Julie was alone.

She felt that her knees would surely buckle under her and she would melt into a mere puddle of fright, but, astonishingly, she was able to walk unassisted when the tenth floor was reached. She stood for a moment, bewildered, looking from right to left down a hall from which glass-paned doors opened.

A young man emerged from another elevator. "Can I help you, Miss?"

Julie gasped out the publisher's name.

"Down the hall and to your left."

"Thank you." Julie hitched up the portfolio and tried to advance boldly because there was nothing else to do.

Double doors opened into an anteroom where a switchboard operator looked at Julie curiously. "Help you?" she drawled.

"I'd like to speak to Miss Helen Graves."

Julie knew Connie's aunt. She had met her at the Blakes' house twice. But as she waited she couldn't recall her features clearly, couldn't even remember the color of her hair. The panic within her grew until lines of strain showed on her face. It seemed incredible that she could have done this thing, could be here at all. Incredible and foolish. She felt appallingly young, like a child in a party dress, and the clicking of typewriters and hushed voices were part of a world in which she had no business. She knew it clearly now.

A tall young woman was walking across the foyer toward her. Julie took a deep breath and met her unrecognizing eyes.

"Miss Graves?"

"Yes, my dear, may I do something for you?"

"I'm Julie Ferguson, a friend of Connie's." Her voice was so low it was almost a whisper.

Miss Graves said without conviction, "Oh, yes, of course."

"Connie said that you were secretary to the art director. I have some drawings. Do you suppose—"

The young woman glanced at the huge portfolio and then at Julie's wide and terrified eyes. She said, smiling at Julie as a grown-up smiles at a child, "You mean, you have some drawings of—*yours*?"

Julie nodded, her hair bobbing on her shoulders. "I thought maybe—"

Miss Graves was looking rather taken aback. "The art director, Mrs. Lytton, is a very busy person," she started, then, at the distress in Julie's eyes, continued, "but I'll see."

Julie thanked her silently.

"Won't you sit down here until I come back?"

Julie sat on the long sofa with her ankles close together. At last, with the aid of a handkerchief and a helpful gush of tears, she got the dust out of her eye. The portfolio, propped against her left knee, shivered slightly. She swallowed again and again. If she could stop trembling, she thought, she would feel better. She wondered if the switchboard operator were noticing.

Miss Graves had disappeared behind one of the glass-paned doors to an inner office. She was gone for several minutes, and Julie watched the door anxiously. It doesn't matter, she told herself. It doesn't matter if she doesn't see me. But now that she had come this far, had crossed so many treacherous hurdles, she knew in her heart that it really did matter. She had to see it through.

Miss Graves came out of the door laughing over her shoulder. "If you'll wait a few minutes, dear, Mrs. Lytton will be able to see you," she said.

"Oh, thank you!"

Why did she keep calling her "my dear" and "dear," Julie wondered. As though she were humoring her, that's the way she talked. As though she were a baby.

A buzz sounded and the switchboard operator adjusted her mouthpiece, murmuring an unintelligible version of the publisher's name into the instrument. Then her expression changed. "Oh, hello, George." Julie listened to the one-sided conversation. "Sure. . . . You're kidding. . . . No I don't. . . . Yeh. . . . Six o'clock? Well, I don't know about six o'clock. Maybe six-thirty, huh? . . . Huh? . . . That's not what you said Saturday night. . . . Look, George, I can't talk now. I'm busy. . . . I said I'm busy. Yeh, I work here, remember? . . . Oh, you! 'Bye now. . . .'Bye."

The place gave Julie a smothering sense of inferiority. So many people, leading such different kinds of lives, all of them busy and self-absorbed. All of them more important by far than she.

"You can come in now." Miss Graves had reappeared. Julie jerked to attention with a pounding heart and knocked the portfolio to the floor with a slap. She picked it up, pulled at the hem of the brown jacket nervously, and did her best to smile.

The click of her own flat heels sounded like whip cracks to Julie as she crossed the room to the art director's door. She heard Miss Graves introduce her—"Julie Ferguson, a friend of my niece's"—and as the latch clicked behind the secretary it seemed to shut out Julie's last tie with the world she recognized.

A voice said: "Good afternoon, Julie. Won't you sit down?" and as Julie slid into a straight oak chair she looked up timidly. "You've brought some drawings for me to look at?" the art director said.

The voice was kind. The woman who spoke was older than Miss Graves, with brown hair swept upward. She wore a severe black dress and her fingernails, though short, were painted a vivid pink. She wasn't in the least pretty, but she looked so sure of herself that Julie found her alarming. She opened her mouth twice to try to speak, and ended by simply shoving the portfolio across the already-littered desk.

Mrs. Lytton untied one tape and Julie fumbled with another. Mrs. Lytton, finishing first, reached for the third. The diamond solitaire on her left hand flashed as she laid the cover back.

The drawings were so small, in the vast portfolio, that they looked ridiculous to Julie. She couldn't watch the art director as she soberly turned the sheets. With her cold hands clasped together in her lap she stared at the walls, decorated with framed illustrations; at the window; at the stack of books piled brightly on a side table; at the floor.

The art director didn't speak until she reached the last of the drawings. Then she turned the entire group back with a single motion and looked up at Julie with a smile that was meant to be encouraging. "Are these your dogs?"

Julie nodded again, wringing her hands in her lap. "At least, well, they *live* at our place."

Mrs. Lytton grew puzzled.

"I mean they're pups from the Lonsdale kennels, really, but they've been boarding out at my dad's farm." Julie flushed, feeling somehow that it was a degrading statement, but Mrs. Lytton seemed interested.

"I've heard of Lonsdale collies," she said, leaning back in her chair.

Not a word about the drawings. *Oh, why don't you talk about the drawings?* Julie willed. *Get it over with, quick!* There was something else, probably, that she herself should say. She should explain about how she had been thinking the drawings might be used in a book.

Like the book she had at home. She should say something like that.

"Aren't they?" asked Mrs. Lytton.

Julie realized that the art director was repeating something she had said before. "I beg your pardon?"

"Aren't they very fine dogs?"

"Oh, yes, very. Especially Sonny." Julie leaned forward. "This is Sonny." She pointed toward the first sketch and her stubby fingers looked travel-grimed next to Mrs. Lytton's carefully manicured hands.

The art director looked down again. "Some of these sketches are very—vigorous," she said thoughtfully, as though she were searching for the proper words. "I can tell you like to draw dogs."

Julie nodded gratefully. She was speechless again but her eyes were very bright.

"They have a lot of action," Mrs. Lytton was going on, still groping for something Julie couldn't comprehend. "Especially the black and whites." She turned a couple of the drawings over again and examined them more minutely. "Are you taking extra art work at school?"

Julie shook her head. "I did these this summer. I thought— sometimes you buy dog drawings for books, don't you?"

Light seemed to break over Mrs. Lytton's face. "We do," she said seriously. "Usually after a manuscript for a dog book is bought, we give it out to an artist, who makes drawings to fit the page size and the text."

"Oh," said Julie.

The art director's voice was sympathetic as she continued. "Usually it's an established artist—someone who has specialized in the field."

The death toll for Julie's hopes rang loud. "I see."

"Though occasionally," Mrs. Lytton went on, very kindly, "we buy illustrations from a young person just out of art school. If the student has talent. If the work fits in with our needs. I hope you're considering going to art school?"

Julie nodded and whispered, "Yes."

"There are good art schools in Philadelphia."

"I'm going to the Academy," Julie said. "My mother went there. She was Margaret Field."

She spoke the name so proudly that Mrs. Lytton replied, "Oh, of course!" and looked down again at the sketches. "I think you'll be very happy at the Academy," she said. "I think you have talent."

The praise felt like fine rain on Julie's head, scarcely reaching her consciousness. Numbly she watched Mrs. Lytton close the portfolio and say, with real warmth, "Will you come to see me after you graduate, Julie? I'd like you to."

Mumbling some inadequate thanks, and without even waiting to tie the portfolio's tapes, Julie fled from the office. It didn't matter that she might have talent. It didn't matter that the art director had been understanding or kind. What mattered was that she was out of that office, on the street again, walking back to the station. Her sense of relief was so immense that she was filled to the brim with it. It pushed her dashed hopes temporarily out of her mind.

That bouncing sense of relief, of escape from a terrible ordeal, lasted all the way home on the train and bus. Julie knew it was synthetic, that actually she had failed, but just to have the physical trauma behind her was enough for the moment. It was so wonderful to be able to breathe again, to be able to come back to dear, familiar Meadowbrook and descend once more the accustomed steps of the bus.

Julie walked up the lane with a step that was almost springy. Then, as she rounded the bend that dropped down to Deepdale's own snug valley, she saw the Lonsdale car, dwarfed by distance, and her father, walking down from the barn with three flashes of gold and white racing ahead of him.

Julie stopped, one hand tightening on the portfolio, the other clutching the top rail of the guard fence.

Not now! Not today! Not after everything else.

Then, with a suddenness that was overpowering, resentment dissolved into despair. Nothing ever turned out right. Nothing, nothing, nothing! The future was unthinkable. Julie couldn't face it.

The instinct to hide from whatever decision Mr. Lonsdale must now be making about the dogs became acutely physical. Ducking behind the trees that lined the path down the hill, Julie began to run. The heavy portfolio banged against her legs and threatened to trip her, but she stumbled along as though she were pursued. On the side of the brook away from the farm buildings was an old springhouse, half hidden under the branches of a guardian tree. A dozen times before it had been an escape, but never had Julie needed its shelter as she did today.

Screened from the yard by a rise of ground, Julie knew that the men couldn't see her as she pushed at the door, swollen from dampness, and slipped inside. The portfolio slid from her hands and settled on the uneven brick floor as, with childish abandon, Julie began to cry. She threw herself full length on the cold bricks and lay face down with her head on her arms. Sobs, unstifled, shattered her. Sonny was lost!

Lost the chance of buying him from Mr. Lonsdale. Lost the dream of keeping him forever for her own. Finally Julie awoke to what the rejection of her drawings meant.

The thought that she might never see Sonny again drove like a spear into her stomach. Yet she couldn't get up and go to him and say good-bye. She hadn't enough courage for that.

"Sonny!" she cried, tight to bursting with emotion, sorry for herself beyond belief. But the springhouse door was shut against her muffled voice and the dogs and men were across the brook and up the winding lane, far away.

When the sun dropped behind the barn the single window of the springhouse darkened. By then Julie was lying quiet on the damp floor. Water, a foot from her head, flowed past her silently, and only the shrill call of the killdeer split the quiet of the place.

"Gurlie, gurlie, gurlie, gurlie." Penetrating and insistent, the repeated chirp beat against Julie's consciousness. "Gurlie, gurlie, gurlie!" She rolled over on her back and the air was cool on her tear-streaked face. "Gurlie, gurlie, gurlie, gurlie."

Julie said, "Oh, shut up."

She turned over again and got to her knees beside the water's run-way. Dipping both hands into the icy stream she brought them up, cup-fashion, to her face. The shock helped. She splashed her face a second time, and with a shuddering, spent sigh rocked back on her heels.

For fully five minutes she sat still, staring at nothing, her hands clenched with the thumbs tucked in, knuckles together, between her knees. If Sonny were gone, right now, no wishing would bring him back. She had to face that fact. No miracle, like selling the drawings, had happened or would happen. Dreaming couldn't make things so.

Julie could see now that the trip to the publisher's office had been a crazy project. She wondered that she could have let her hopes run so wild. "Wishful thinking," Dad always called it. Only she had never translated it into action before.

Well, what was done was done. And the future, no matter how furiously she tried to deny it, had to be borne. She reached for her purse and took out tissues to blow her swollen nose.

The Lonsdale car was gone when Julie opened the springhouse door. There was no sign of her father. No dogs were barking. The farm, as the September day lengthened into early twilight, sprawled out in quiet peace. There would be dinner to get and Julie was already late, yet her steps dragged as she walked back to the bridge and up the lane toward the house.

Tom Ferguson was standing by the kitchen window turning the pages of the daily newspaper. Julie could see him from the stoop. He grunted as he heard the door open, but he went right on reading, even when Julie came into the kitchen and turned on the water faucet behind his back.

Julie filled the teakettle and lighted the gas stove. Finally she could put off the question no longer. "Dad, what about the pups?"

"Cocoa's been sold to a fine kennel in Connecticut," Tom said, still not turning. Julie could tell from the emphasis of his voice that he too hated to lose the dogs. "Sistie goes to a Chicago breeder—"

"Sonny?" Julie whispered, not waiting for him to finish.

"For the time being, Sonny stays with us."

Julie's sigh of pure relief made her father turn. "For the time being," he repeated.

"I know, Dad." Yet she couldn't help the wave of joy that swept her. The delay, no matter how brief, was almost too good to be true. While the vegetables were cooking she raced out to the barn and flung her arms eagerly around the big puppy's neck.

"I'm so glad," she told him. "Sonny, I'm so glad!"

The collie seemed glad, too. He rubbed his cold nose into Julie's neck and pawed at her shoulder. His brother and sister were strangely absent and more than ever before he needed Julie's love.

Tom declared that now Sonny could spend the greater part of his time unconfined. That very evening he brought him up to the house after supper, and while he combed and brushed him he talked to Julie about his points.

"Look at those forelegs. Straight as an arrow. See how he stands up on his toes, and feel that spring of rib. Mr. Lonsdale didn't make a mistake, keepin' Sonny. He's going to be a mighty fine dog."

Julie crouched on the floor and followed the movement of her father's hands. She watched him trace the dark mask that outlined the collie's almond eyes and listened to his praise of the dog's head.

"Rounded muzzle but not veiny; that's as it should be. Narrow between the eyes." He whistled suddenly, then at Sonny's response shouted: "And just look at those ears, girl! He'll never need lead in those."

Julie kept nodding. "Will he be a champion, d'you think?"

"His mother was, and so was his father. And for my money, Sonny tops the two of them."

As her father talked, Julie suddenly began to see Sonny in a new light. He was her companion, her beloved friend, but she knew now, and didn't fight the knowing, that someday Mr. Lonsdale would take Sonny away. She realized that there would be essential justice in the parting, that Sonny was born to a great heritage. Her father, who had made no mention of her swollen eyes, was making her understand how rare a champion show dog is, and Julie knew beyond question of doubt that Sonny would be one of the best.

"We can start training him soon," Tom said.

"To stand properly, to walk and run on leash, to obey standard commands. There's a lot you can do to help."

Julie was more than willing. It gave her a new sense of responsibility, a new interest in life. She watched her father work with the dog, then tried to copy his technique. It seemed to Julie that Sonny obeyed her more readily than he did the man. Tom thought so, too.

"That's natural," he said. "He feels you're his mistress. He knows your voice and touch better than mine."

Later, after Sonny had been returned to the kennel, and when Julie was ready to go upstairs to bed, she said to her dad: "I skipped school this afternoon. I've got to have you write me a note."

She braced herself to answer her father's questions, and was astonished when he didn't ask, "Why?"

"All right," he said. "You write it and I'll sign it." It was as easy as that.

The very next morning Sonny started following Julie to the school bus, and when she reached home in the afternoon there he was again, sitting by the R.D. box and staring down the road hopefully as the vehicle swayed and rattled toward him. When Julie dismounted he was wild with joy. He cantered around her barking, his eyes bright with welcome, his tail wagging briskly. From then on escorting her to and from the bus was his daily custom. Though she was reconciled to losing him, more than ever before Sonny was Julie's dog.

Once the die concerning Sonny was finally cast, Julie began to awake to what it meant to be a sophomore. For one thing, the girls seemed casually friendly. Perhaps it was because Julie wasn't trying so hard to make them like her; the concentration she had centered on her trip to Philadelphia with the drawings had made her less socially self-conscious among them. They misinterpreted her detachment, thinking it was self-confidence, and therefore they treated her with a certain respect.

The entire school, about this time, was excited about tryouts for *H.M.S. Pinafore*. It was to be an ambitious venture, grander than anything Meadowbrook High had ever before presented, and even Julie went about humming the catchy Gilbert and Sullivan music in an absent-minded monotone.

She didn't know the words, but the tunes, played over and over again for embryo Captains, Boatswains, Sir Josephs, and Little Buttercups, drifted in from the music room to the study hall, where Julie was regularly scheduled to spend the last period in the afternoon. They were peppy, spirited, and delightfully out of character with the snow that now lay piled high under the black-branched trees that lined Meadowbrook's streets. They gave school an atmosphere of perpetual *fiesta*, and a desire to be part of the fun began again to stir in Julie, although she couldn't sing a note.

Dick was planning to try out for the Captain's part. Every morning Julie could hear him before she could see him, booming the lyrics in a vigorous voice as he slid down the icy road to meet the school bus.

> *"I am never known to quail*
> *At the fury of a gale,*
>   *And I'm never, never sick at sea!"*

"What, never?" Julie learned to call.

"No, never!" Dick would shout back.

"What, *never?*"

"Hardly ever!"

Julie hoped Dick wouldn't be disappointed. She herself thought his voice was pretty good, except when it cracked from growing pains. But Dick was only a sophomore, and lunchroom gossip had it that most of the leads would go to seniors and juniors. She mentioned this to Dick.

The boy nodded but shrugged. "Might as well shoot for the top," he said. "It's easier to climb down than up."

Both Connie and Anne hoped to make the chorus. They had voices that were true but small, and they realized, along with everyone else, that they would have to count largely on their looks to see them through. Fat little Sue Downs surprised Julie by announcing after gym class one day that she intended to screw up her courage and see if she couldn't get the Little Buttercup role. Sidney and Anne were equally surprised when they heard it. Sidney raised her eyebrows meaningfully, and from then on the idea seemed to be discarded in everybody's mind except Sue's.

The piano in the music room banged on every afternoon for two weeks, and gradually contestants for the major roles were narrowed down. Everybody in Julie's crowd had Bob Hartman, the football captain, picked for the Sir Joseph role, but when the list of leads was finally posted they found it had gone to a tall, quiet boy named Hartje Vane whom nobody had ever heard of at all!

But the biggest surprise—the news that rocked the sophomore girls back on their heels and then made them glow with belated pride when they recovered—was that Sue Downs would play Little Buttercup.

Sue couldn't believe it. She fought her way through the pushing crowd around the bulletin board until she could see the notice herself.

Little Buttercup . . . . . . Susan Downs.

There it was, in black and white. Julie, watching Sue's astonished face, was so glad for her she could have cried.

Sue caught her eye and grinned disarmingly. "I guess it's because I'm fat," she giggled, and wandered off to accept congratulations in a happy trance.

Dick's name wasn't among the leads. Julie rode home on the bus with him the afternoon the list was posted. She tried to be very gentle and comforting because he had failed to get not only the coveted Captain's part but the secondary role of Dick Deadeye, for which he had also tried.

But Dick seemed far from downhearted. "I'm in the chorus, aren't I?" he asked. "Wait'll you see me in a sailor suit! Boy, will I be something?" Right in the bus aisle he started to do a hornpipe, clowning.

> *"We sail the ocean blue,*
> *And our saucy ship's a beauty;*
> *We're sober men and true,*
> *And attentive to our duty."*

Julie, too intense to be an easy loser, smiled at him admiringly. "I wish I could sing—or something."

"You can. Something, I mean. You can draw."

Julie looked at the boy. "You mean costumes?" She shook her head. "I can't sew a straight stitch."

"What about stage sets?"

But Julie, remembering that Rodney Post, president of the senior class, was chairman of the scenery committee, again shook her head.

Yet the urge to contribute something of herself to the all-school project kept nudging at Julie. The operetta seemed so colorful and so glamorous that she couldn't help wanting to be part of it. Anne had been chosen for the chorus, though Connie had lost out, and every lunch hour Julie took her tray to the same table with Sue and Anne, in an effort to be closer to the center of things.

Conversation, temporarily discarding the time-honored subject of boys, centered busily around the school play. Sidney was subchairman of the ticket committee and acted very important about it. Sue was steeped in a strange combination of stage fright and bliss. Anne was very chorus-minded.

"I'd rather be in the chorus than have a lead," she told everyone. "It's not so scary and it's more fun."

The most unexpected people blossomed overnight as one committee after another was organized. The operetta somehow lent a new character to the school. It was a project in which ability counted more than popularity, although frequently Julie noticed that the two went hand in hand. Celebrities, previously confined to class officers and football men, now included all the main characters of *H.M.S. Pinafore*. Look at Sue Downs! She was enjoying a prestige beyond her wildest dreams. Buttercup was a somebody in the sophomore class!

Sue's unexpected rise to fame indirectly encouraged Julie. She began to hope that she would be appointed to some committee that had to do with sets or props, and scanned the lists timidly as they were posted, one after another, on the bulletin board.

But her name was never among them. Nobody at the head of things had ever heard of Julie Ferguson. Nobody, except Miss Farrell, even knew she could draw. Well, to be fair, Julie included Dick with Miss Farrell. He kept prodding her.

"Why don't you go to Rod Post and tell him you want to help paint sets?" he urged her. "He really needs people like you."

When Julie shook her head he said, "I'll tell him then."

"Oh, no!" Julie looked really alarmed. "Don't you dare, Dick Webster!" Yet later she almost hoped he would.

The word went around, at the beginning of rehearsals, that the coach wanted the cast to stop singing the *H.M.S. Pinafore* music around school, so that the tunes wouldn't seem stale when the operetta was finally produced. From then on everything was very hush-hush, and more exciting than ever.

A committee of carpenters was building the hull of a boat right on the auditorium stage, across which the red velvet curtains were now continually drawn. The front, with a magnificent masthead, stuck out at one end and the stern at the other. The principal had to conduct assembly from a table on the auditorium floor.

One morning he made an announcement that caused Julie to prick up her ears. The art department was sponsoring a poster contest for *H.M.S. Pinafore*. Entrants were invited to register with Miss Farrell and would be permitted to attend a rehearsal of the first act, which was as far as the cast had yet gone. Every entrant was then honor-bound to submit a poster, and the winner would automatically become chairman of the poster committee for the show, as well as winning a ten-dollar cash prize.

Julie registered, as much because she was wild with curiosity to see a rehearsal of the operetta as because she had an interest in the contest. Along with sixteen other entrants, mostly girls, she sat in the back row of the auditorium one afternoon while an appearance of order among the sprawling cast was achieved by the hard-working coach.

The hull of the good ship, half completed, reared innocent of paint to enclose the chorus of sailors, who all worked lazily as they sang the opening strains of "We Sail the Ocean Blue." Julie especially watched Dick, who seemed to be scrambling down the ropes or doing something of the sort, looking as little like a sailor, in his worn blue jeans, as any of them.

She completely missed the entrance of Little Buttercup. Suddenly there was Sue, round and rosy, in a too-tight sweater and a short plaid skirt, with an empty wicker basket as her only prop. The music changed to waltz time as Sue walked forward timidly, and Julie's mouth dropped open as she started to sing.

> *"I'm called Little Buttercup, dear Little Buttercup,*
> *Though I could never tell why,*
> *But still I'm called Buttercup, poor Little Buttercup,*
> *Sweet Little Buttercup I!"*

Her soprano was sweet and true, just right for the lilting, foolish air. It seemed incredible to Julie that it was Sue standing there, singing all alone—little Sue Downs, whom she knew as well as she knew any girl in the sophomore class.

> *"I've snuff and tobaccy, and excellent jacky,*
> *I've scissors, and watches, and knives;*
> *I've ribbons and laces to set off the faces*
> *Of pretty young sweethearts and wives."*

As Sue started showing the sailors her wares, Julie forgot the sweater and skirt she wore and clothed her in the cap and apron, beruffled and beribboned, that the character should have worn. From

84

then on she sat enchanted, swayed by Sullivan's contagious music, straining her ears to hear every word of the songs.

> *"A maiden fair to see,*
> *The pearl of minstrelsy,*
> *A bud of blushing beauty . . ."*

Julie saw the singer, not in her school clothes but in an Empire frock with puffed sleeves, a parasol over her head, and Ralph Rackstraw on his knees at her feet. And when Sir Joseph, a dapper boy who twirled an invisible moustache, announced, "'I am the monarch of the sea,'" she immediately pictured him in the proper Napoleonic hat. All the costume prints that had been hung for weeks around the art classroom came to life. What a poster could be done for this show!

She caught the late bus home, and all the way to the farm the music kept going round and round in her head. She sang it to Sonny, who came racing up to the ridge at the sound of the bus brakes, as they walked to the house together through the snow.

> *"I am the captain of the* Pinafore! . . .
> *And a right good captain, too!"*

But that night, when she tried to put the Captain on paper in a preliminary poster sketch, he wouldn't come alive for her. She couldn't capture the gaiety, the nonsense quality, of the operetta, though she was full of its atmosphere and tried her level best.

She had a week to work on the poster, but a week seemed too short. She discarded sketch after sketch, and finally, despairing of preliminary black-and-white drawings, tried working directly in show card colors on gray cardboard. That technique seemed better, but it still wasn't what she was looking for. She wanted to do a poster that would carry the joyous spirit of the comic opera, that would make the characters dance right across the room, that would make them sing!

One afternoon after school she walked down to the Meadowbrook Public Library looking for ideas, and went through every book about Gilbert and Sullivan she could find. Finally she found what she wanted—a group of drawings so blinding bright, so jolly, so simple and whimsical, that even the author and composer, she thought, would have loved them.

If she could do something like that!

Yet she couldn't copy; she could only try to imitate the spirit, the paper-doll look of them.

Paper! The thought crystallized in her mind. Characters cut from bright and shiny paper, mounted on poster board.

At the stationery store next to the movies she found the kind of thin, shiny paper kindergarten children use. The sheets weren't large, but they were magenta, crimson, yellow, and electric blue. She spent the last of her week's lunch money on paper and paste and took them home with her.

The next morning she left a penciled note for Mrs. Mott.

Dear Mrs. Mott—
Will you please fix something easy for supper tonight and tomorrow night? I will be awfully busy both times.

Thank you,
Julie.

She snipped and cut with an absorption that excluded, not only her dad, but also Sonny. The collie lay under the round kitchen table at which his mistress worked and felt scraps of paper drift down onto his head like falling leaves. He saw Julie's thin legs wound around the rungs of the chair. Occasionally her toes wiggled in her sneakers, and then he looked up, hoping she would stop whatever she was doing and play with him, but for once Sonny didn't come first.

Tom looked at the mess with mild curiosity. "What's that you're doing, Julie?"

"Trying to make a poster for *H.M.S. Pinafore*! They're giving it at school."

"*Pinafore*, eh?" The man stood with his hands in the pockets of his old tweed jacket and stared down at the table. "I'd kind of like to hear that music again. It's got a beat to it. We heard the D'Oyle Carte people do it once."

Julie knew that the "we" included her mother, though Tom seldom mentioned Margaret directly. Unexpectedly she said, "You could go with me."

The words were no sooner spoken than she regretted them. How would she look, appearing with her father, when all the rest of the girls would probably have dates? But then the pleased expression on Tom's face made her ashamed, and she forced herself to say: "Why don't you, Dad? Dick's going to be a chorus boy. I think it would be fun."

Tom grinned down at her. "Might do that," he said. He walked out of the room whistling a tune from the score.

It started to snow at dusk the night before the poster was due. Julie worked very late on the lettering, and when she finally went to bed, her eyes burned with fatigue. She had worked with such concentration that she had lost all critical sense about the job. It was bright. It was certainly different. It could be seen from a considerable distance. But whether the poster was really good or just odd, Julie simply couldn't tell.

She awoke in the morning feeling apprehensive. It was still snowing, so she had to wrap her entry in a covering of old newspapers in order to protect it when she took it to school. The wind was blowing from the road, and she walked backward up the lane, holding the parcel flat against her body so it wouldn't blow. She was fearful, because the snow was wet and sticky and it would be dreadful if the poster were to be streaked.

She unpacked it on a table in the art classroom. Several other contestants were there, too, unwrapping their entries or looking at those already hung against the walls. The biggest group was around a poster by Marcia Redding, a senior who was art editor of Meadowbrook's school paper, *Blade*.

Julie could hear the comments.

"Marcia, that's wonderful!"

"Boy, you've got it sewed up and ticketed."

"Come here and look at this one, Jane. Isn't this great?"

Marcia was a popular girl and her friends hurried to praise her. Julie's heart sank. What had she been thinking of, anyway, to believe for a minute that she might come out on top? She scolded herself mentally for such daydreaming. The experience with the dog drawings should have taught her a lesson. She mustn't even allow herself to hope.

Yet she was relieved, when she unfolded the newspapers, to find the poster unharmed. Not that it especially pleased her this morning. The lettering, at which she was least able, seemed uneven, the composition too simple and childish, compared with the more complicated posters that were visible from where she stood. The cutouts, however, were certainly colorful. The full skirts of Buttercup stood away from the board to show frilled undies made of lace-doily paper and Sir Joseph's cocked hat boasted a real feather. But all the other posters were painted. Suppose, because this was made of cutouts, it disqualified her. There she was, hoping again! As though she really had a chance at the prize.

Julie rolled up the damp newspapers and stuffed them in the wastebasket. She tried to get a glimpse of Marcia Redding's poster, but the crowd around it was too thick. Leaving her own poster on the table, Julie slipped out of the room.

All day she practiced self-discipline. She refused to let herself think about the contest at all. She made a special effort not to be alone, to join one or another of the girls on their way to or from class, to get at a crowded table in the lunchroom. But the subject of the poster would come up. As soon as she had disposed of her tray and settled down on her stool, Anne mentioned it.

"You've got a poster in the contest, haven't you, Julie?"

Julie nodded. "Uh-huh."

Shirley Graham, who was sitting beside Anne, looked across the table at her and yawned. "I hear Marcia Redding's is a wow."

"It must be," Julie said, making her voice enthusiastic. "There was such a gang around it this morning you couldn't get near it."

Connie said, "What's yours like, Julie?"

Julie pretended she didn't hear, but Connie was insistent. "What's yours like, Julie?"

"It's cutouts."

"Cutouts?" Shirley repeated, questioning.

Julie wished they'd talk about something else. "The figures are cut out of paper instead of being painted."

Connie and Anne both looked interested. Anne said, "That sounds like fun."

Julie said, "I don't know. I thought it was while I was working on it but now I really don't know."

Sun glistened on the heavy snow that blanketed Deepdale and fell warm on Julie's bare head as she stood looking down from the ridge. The sky, for the first time in three days, was blue, and looked innocent of its recent downpouring of flakes that had not fallen softly, but had hurried, in lines barely slanting against the dark trunks of the maple trees.

Now that it was clear again, the farm emerged in fancy dress. The two boxwoods by the stoop wore great peaked hats of snow. The pines were dressed in scalloped layers of it, heavy white ball gowns embroidered in green. Snow was blanketed on the chimneys, swept in whipped-cream drifts against the barn. It garnished the dead field grass by the brook and blossomed on the dogwood. It was the most becoming snow Julie had ever seen.

"Son-ny!" She cupped her hands to her mouth, called, and waited. Today, of all days, she wanted to share with the collie. She wanted to shout and to run, though running was out of the question, for the fluff was deceptively deep. "Sonny!"

Ah! That was why he hadn't met her. He'd been shut up with her dad inside the barn. But he was coming now, bounding through the whiteness, head up, tail wagging, straining to get to her as quickly as he could.

"Take it easy, boy! I'll wait for you." But instead of waiting Julie started down the ridge to meet the dog. They reached each other breathless, and Julie let her schoolbooks slide out of her lap as she crouched to gather Sonny in her arms, crushing his snow-spangled ruff against her coat.

"What d'you think, Sonny?" She *had* to tell him. "I won the prize."

Once said, although Sonny couldn't understand, the remarkable fact seemed doubly true.

The collie recognized the happiness in her voice. He licked her face, nibbled at her mittens, rolled over on his back in the deep softness, and barked in unconstrained joy.

Julie smiled down at him and rubbed his belly. Then, as he scrambled to his feet, she picked up her books and banged them together to rid them of the clinging snow. Sonny trotted ahead of her as she picked a path on down the hill.

She was still smiling when she reached the house. In the yard she paused for a minute to wade through a drift to her homemade bird-feeding station, where snow banked on the platform was confounding the hungry cardinals. She swooped it off with a single gesture and said, "There!"

But she wasn't really thinking about what she was doing. She was reliving the day. She would never forget it—never!—though it seemed scarcely real. She could feel again the emptiness of her stomach as the principal started to make the announcement. She could see his sandy eyebrows work up and down as they always did when he strained his voice to make himself heard.

"Now we come to the matter of the poster contest . . ."

Julie had kept her eyes straight in front of her. She had tried not to wiggle. She had pretended disinterest.

"First I want to say that all the entries have merit. The judges consider the creative ability of the contestants remarkably high."

Oh, go on, go on, Mr. Stewart, Julie had willed. She felt as she had when Mrs. Lytton looked through her drawings, as though if the decision didn't come soon she'd burst. *If it's Marcia Redding, say so. Hurry!* Julie had seen Marcia's poster by now. It was good—very good. But she felt deep inside that hers was pretty good, too. So did Anne and Connie. With real respect in their voices, they had told her so. "Wouldn't it be wonderful," they'd said, "if a sophomore should win!"

"There were sixteen posters submitted, and the judges used as a basis of scoring . . ."

Wouldn't it be wonderful! No, don't let yourself. Something in

90

Julie's insides was turning cartwheels. Then, out of the fog of words surrounding Mr. Stewart, she heard her name.

"Julie Ferguson."

Her name. Her name! Anne, on her left, was squeezing her arm, and the student body was clapping courteously.

"Julie! Julie—it's you!"

Julie couldn't smile. Her lips felt dry and parched.

"You have to go up front and get the prize, Julie." Anne was giving her a gentle push.

She couldn't. She couldn't go up there in front of the whole school. But somehow, weak-kneed, she did. Feeling all arms and legs, feeling awkward and embarrassed and yet somehow very proud, she took the envelope from the principal and mumbled her thanks.

Scurrying back to her seat, she almost tripped over Dick Webster's foot, stretched out into the side aisle. "Hot stuff, Peanut!" he whispered as she was brought up short.

Color flooded her cheeks. She didn't know whether he was praising her or kidding her. She slipped into her seat again, trembling, and stared down at the envelope in her lap.

Feeling again the wonder and the terror of it all, Julie looked back over the day as she hung her coat on one of the wooden pegs in the hall. Sonny, sensing her mood, rubbed against Julie's skirt and looked up at her, trying to bring her back to the present by asking for a caress.

Absently, Julie stroked the collie's head. There was so much now to think about and to plan. Being chairman of the poster committee loomed as a big responsibility. She had never been chairman of anything before.

Members would have to be appointed. She'd better ask Miss Farrell about that. Arrangements would have to be made to place posters in the station, the drugstore, the post office, and a dozen different places. Art materials would have to be bought and paid for. Money would have to be set aside from the play budget. Gradually Julie began to sense the challenges of her new job.

Tom came in, knocking his feet together to clear them of snow. Julie told him about the prize at once, breathlessly.

"Dad, you know that poster I was doing? For the contest?"

91

Tom grunted affirmatively. He was rubbing his cold hands, shrugging off his Mackinaw, not paying much attention.

"I won the prize." Julie tried to say it modestly but she couldn't help sounding proud. She took the envelope out of her coat pocket and displayed the ten-dollar bill. "See?"

The money awakened Tom's notice where her words hadn't. "You won that? Good for you!"

He walked past her into the kitchen and picked up the mail which Julie had brought from the R.D. box. Julie was disappointed that her father wasn't more impressed. She trailed after him, wanting to tell him all about the way the prize had happened, but Tom was frowning at the telephone bill, too occupied to give her much attention. Julie felt a little let down.

Not for long, though. She hummed as she went about the routine of preparing supper, and it never occurred to Julie, as she poured milk into the big, old-fashioned tumblers, that for the first time in ages she was looking forward to the next day at school.

Julie loved the sense of busyness, of importance, of being part of things, that her new position gave her. She tried to go forward carefully so she would make no missteps, and she consulted Miss Farrell before she appointed her committee members.

The art teacher was sympathetic and helpful, suggesting that Julie choose five of the contest entrants to serve. Julie was entirely agreeable. Only when Marcia Redding's name came up did she object.

"She's a senior and everything. Maybe she wouldn't want to."

Miss Farrell looked at Julie quizzically. "Why not? Just because she didn't win the prize?" She shook her head firmly. "Marcia's not like that."

Yet Julie approached Marcia with considerable shyness. She showed obvious surprise and pleasure when the older girl said, "Certainly I'll work on your committee, Julie. I'd like to."

Marcia did a lot for Julie. She gave her self-confidence a boost. She was aggressive and able and she had a manner of talking to shopkeepers that got more posters into more places than Julie could ever have managed alone. Julie admired her intensely. She tried to copy Marcia's forthright manner, her definite way of speaking, even the hearty good nature of her laugh. Of course the result was very little like Marcia Redding, but it did give Julie a sense of being more of a person, even if the person was not quite herself.

It was Marcia's idea to take posters to some of the suburban towns surrounding Meadowbrook. "People who like Gilbert and Sullivan," she said, "will come—even to an amateur performance that isn't put on by local talent. I think it would pay."

Julie and her committee made twenty new posters, all of them copied from her original technique, and they began to bloom in store windows and in the corridors of public buildings near and far. It gave Julie a peculiar new thrill of accomplishment to walk into the post office to mail a letter and see one of her posters on the wall. She was delighted when two women stopped and commented on it. She hoped beyond words that the auditorium would be jam-packed on all three nights of the show.

All committee chairmen got their tickets free, but out of her ten dollars' prize money Julie bought a ticket for her father, and gave it to him, along with a white linen handkerchief, on his birthday a week before the show.

On the Thursday of the opening Mr. Stewart announced at assembly that the play was a sellout. "We have the ticket committee and the poster committee to thank," he said appreciatively, and Julie sat with her hands clenched in her lap, ready to burst with pride.

It seemed to her, during these weeks, that she was more welcome in the crowd of sophomore girls she knew best than she had been since grammar-school days. She was so happy and so busy with her new responsibilities that she smiled a lot, just at anybody she happened to meet—anybody at all. She dashed through her lunches so that she could get in half an hour's work in the art classroom, where the poster committee gathered. She didn't care whom she ate with or whether she ate alone, yet Anne and Shirley and Connie and Sue always seemed to congregate at the same table, and were usually only half through their sandwiches when Julie was ready to leave.

She'd say, "'Bye now," with her mouth still full, and push back her chair as she spoke. "What's your hurry, Julie?" Anne asked one day, pretending to frown. "Sit down and relax, can't you?" But Julie just shook her head and grinned.

Now that she didn't seek companionship, now that she didn't care whether Anne was really scolding her or only teasing, it seemed to Julie that everyone was remarkably friendly. It must be, she thought, because of the poster business. When *Pinafore* is over and forgotten, things will go back again to the way they used to be.

But she was ready to take advantage of her good fortune while it lasted. She was ready to return friendliness with friendliness, and to do her best to overcome her shyness and meet any overtures more than halfway.

She rarely saw Dick. He was busy with rehearsals and she with her posters after school. He walked over to Deepdale one Saturday morning, to return a tool he had borrowed from her dad, and caught Julie with her hair done up in rollers, blocking a sweater on the kitchen table and whistling tunelessly to herself.

"Hi, Peanut," he said from the door.

Julie whirled around, suddenly self-conscious. Her hands flew to her head. "Hi." She sounded annoyed.

Dick's eyes followed her gesture. "Caught you at it, huh? So that's what it takes to give a gal glamour." He slurred the word, grinning, and shook his head. "A fine thing!"

Julie could feel herself blushing. "You could've knocked," she snapped. She turned back to the sweater, poking at the wet wool energetically.

Dick walked into the room, hands in his pockets, circled the table so that he again faced her, and sat down. He stretched and yawned. "Well, next week's the play," he said. "After that I get some sleep."

Julie said, mocking his self-importance. "Oh, you poor dear!"

Dick chuckled. "Now we're even. Come on, Julie, forget your hair. Don't get mad."

Julie grinned back, reluctantly. After all, Dick was an old friend. He probably didn't even look at her as a girl, the way he did at Connie. She supposed she was silly to care.

They talked about the operetta for a while. "Wait till you see Hartje Vane," Dick told her, full of admiration. "That guy's a discovery. I mean it. He's meat for a Hollywood talent scout."

Julie took the praise with a grain of salt, but she rather liked Dick's exaggeration. She felt an almost personal pride in Hartje Vane's success. Up to a few weeks ago he had been a nobody, like herself.

His swift climb to fame meant to Julie that she and all other nobodies also had a chance.

"What night you going?" she heard Dick ask.

"Friday."

He nodded. "That'll be the best night. Thursday we'll be scared and Saturday we'll be tired."

But Saturday would be date night, Julie knew. Saturday would be the most fun, no matter whether the cast was tired or not. She wondered whether Dick had a date for after the show. It made her remember her hair again, and the awful way she must look. She couldn't think of anything else to say and she couldn't keep patting at the sweater much longer.

Dick jerked his head toward the door. "Your dad just told me you're going to drag him along."

Julie could feel the red sliding up her neck and the more she tried to stop it the faster the heat seemed to climb to her cheeks. Now why did her father have to tell Dick that? Why did he have to advertise, practically, that she didn't have a date? She kept her head down and nodded. "Uh-huh. He wants to see what you look like in bell-bottomed pants."

Dick laughed. "Instead of overalls. He told me." Suddenly he turned serious. "I think he's tickled pink about your taking him, but he wouldn't admit it for a million bucks."

Julie looked up. "D'you really?"

Dick nodded. "He's a good guy, your pop."

Julie's glance thanked him. "Sometimes he's sort of hard to talk to."

"For a girl, maybe. Not for a fellow."

Dick's praise made Julie take to glancing at her father secretly, trying to see what made the boy hold him in such high regard. He looked much the same as always, lean, hard, the skin above the collar of his wool shirt tanned the year round, crow's feet branching out in thin lines from the outer corners of his deep-set eyes. But Dick's words had changed him, nevertheless, made him a man's man. Maybe it shouldn't matter that she couldn't seem to talk to him much.

The Friday night on which they drove in to Meadowbrook to see *Pinafore* was icy and cold. Tom shaved in the kitchen after dinner as a concession to the occasion, but he came downstairs, ready to leave, dressed in slacks and a tweed jacket rather than the good blue suit Julie had expected him to wear. She was disappointed. He looked rough and "country," she thought, but she knew better than to question his choice.

During the ride along the half-cleared highway, Julie was wondering how her father would appear to her school friends, and whether, after all, he would really like the play. She could feel herself growing critical and uneasy on both counts. She almost wished she were back home.

But once they were settled in their seats in the high-school auditorium, led there by an usher in a long and swishy dress, Julie began to relax. It hadn't been too bad. Not many people had greeted them, and to the one introduction she had felt called upon to make her father had responded with an easy smile.

When the curtain rose at last, she forgot everything but the spirit and music of the comic opera. Only once did she lean toward her father, to whisper, "That's Sue Downs, a friend of mine." For the remainder of act one she sat entranced, her hands clasped in her lap, her eyes shining, recurrently swept by astonishment that the actors and actresses on the stage were actually people she knew!

She clapped automatically with the rest of the audience but when the lights went on for the intermission she blinked, finding it hard to return to reality. Her father, who had also been applauding enthusiastically, was less overwhelmed.

"You kids do a good job," he said, including Julie flatteringly. Then he began to fidget and look around. "I want a smoke. Let's get out of here."

Julie didn't know where fathers might be allowed to smoke. She thought downstairs, maybe, and followed her dad's broad back out of the auditorium. Laughter and conversation buzzed up the stairwell, and, still following, she joined the exodus from the auditorium toward the ground floor.

Gordon Wyatt and Connie Blake passed her in the corridor, nodded and smiled. "Swell, isn't it?" Connie asked.

"Swell!" echoed Julie.

Dr. Harper, the veterinarian, and his plump, dowdy wife were wedged in by the drinking fountain. Tom Ferguson waved. "Hi, Doc!" his big voice boomed.

"Hi, Tom. How's things at the farm?"

"Fine as silk. Fine as silk."

Heads turned and Julie felt uncomfortably conscipuous. She tried to hurry her dad on.

At the bottom of the stairs Miss Farrell approached them, smiling. "Good evening, Julie. Quite a crowd those posters drew!"

Tom looked down at his daughter and said in a carrying whisper, "Teacher of yours?"

Julie was trapped. "This is my father, Miss—" she started to stumble.

But the art teacher was ahead of her, easy and gracious. "I'm Linda Farrell, Mr. Ferguson. I suppose you know you've got a daughter with real art ability here." She smiled at Julie.

Why, Miss Farrell looks like a girl tonight, Julie was thinking, instead of listening to her words. She had never realized how young the teacher must be—in her twenties, probably. She watched her now with new curiosity, noticing how Miss Farrell's long eyelashes touched her cheeks as she looked up at Julie's dad.

"Have I now?" Tom was saying, his eyes interested, crinkling at the corners. But it occurred to Julie that he, no more than she, was listening to Miss Farrell's actual words.

"Haven't you seen her posters? They're plastered all over town." Criticism tinged the teacher's voice.

Tom looked embarrassed. "I guess I haven't," he said sheepishly. "I don't get in from the farm much."

Like a country hick, Julie thought. Oh, Dad!

But Miss Farrell didn't seem to mind. She shook her head in dismay but her eyes were smiling. "You fathers! Anyway, I'm going to ride out to the farm someday and have a talk with you about this little girl." Her lashes lowered, then lifted. "That is, if I may?"

Now what can she mean by that, Julie was wondering. She scarcely heard her father say, warmly, "Of course you may!" before they were swept on with the crowd. Then, almost at once, the ushers were shouting, "Second act curtain in five minutes," and she and her father were walking upstairs again to get to their seats.

"Pretty girl, that," Tom said, as he settled himself.

"Who?" Julie looked around.

"Your Miss Farrell."

"Oh. Yes. She's nice, too."

Dick, still streaked with grease paint, rode home with Julie and her dad.

It was none of Julie's doing. She and her father had edged their way out of the milling crowd in the high-school corridors and on the broad front steps and were already seated in the Ford when Dick and a couple of other boys from the cast strolled past, whistling. Before Julie could stop him Tom Ferguson tooted his horn and leaned out his side of the car.

"Dick!"

"Hi, Mr. Ferguson!"

Julie shrank back against the seat, out of the ray of the street lamp. Dick stopped and his companions walked idly on.

"Want a lift?"

Dick looked briefly after his friends, then decided. "Sure."

Tom reached across Julie and opened the car door. Julie edged over toward her dad and Dick climbed in. "Hi, Peanut," he said.

"Hello, Dick." Tom, now concentrating on warming up the spluttering, choking old car, seemed oblivious to any responsibility for further conversation, so Julie added, "The show was swell."

Dick was full of it. "Boy, did you see me in the second act! I nearly took a header. Tripped over that coil of rope in the middle of 'Carefully on Tiptoe Stealing.' Boy, would my name have been mud! Can't you imagine 'em singing, 'Goodness me! Why, what was that?' and instead of 'Silent be, It was the cat!' having me hit the deck? Whew!"

Tom and Julie both laughed and Tom started to sing the song in his rumbling bass.

> *"Carefully on tiptoe stealing,*
> *Breathing gently as we may,*
> *Every step with caution feeling,*
> *We will softly steal away."*

"Why, Dad," Julie said, "you know all the words!"

Dick joined him and together they roared out the chorus as the car bucked down the icy street. It was noisy, but it was fun. Julie felt herself grinning, tingling with the thrill the *H.M.S. Pinafore* music always inspired. Both Dick and her father were in high spirits, and they couldn't stop with one tune. They sang "Never Mind the Why and Wherefore" and "When I Was a Lad," Tom filling in with "da-da-da" when he forgot a few lines. Dick attempted "Refrain, Audacious Tar," but Tom balked at that. It was too high for him.

"Come on, Julie. You sing." Dick nudged the girl's shoulder.

Julie shook her head. "I can't carry a tune even." But she hummed along with them in a whispering monotone. She couldn't resist doing that.

Tom drove Dick right on up to his own house, which was built much closer to the main road than Deepdale. "Thanks, Mr. Ferguson. This is real service!" Dick said as he climbed out. "See you tomorrow, Ju?"

"Tomorrow?" Tomorrow was Saturday.

"At school, I mean. You know there's a dance after the show tomorrow night."

"Oh, yes. Of course." Julie spoke stupidly, trying to fill in the silence with something other than, "I don't think I'll be going." The vague answer, fortunately, seemed to satisfy Dick. He raced up the porch steps two at a time, then stood at the top watching the car as it negotiated the turnaround.

"'Bye now!"

"'Bye," Julie called back, making her voice bright, but as they eased off the highway into Deepdale's long lane she felt a little let down.

The next morning, to take her mind off the dance to which she would not be going, Julie helped Mrs. Mott clean the attic. It was a thankless job, and dirty. She tied her hair in a torn piece of sheet and put on her oldest jeans.

Sonny followed her up the stairs, but before many minutes had passed he was choking with the dust and willing enough to be ordered out to the sparkling cold sunlight. "This isn't a gentleman's job," Julie told him. "After lunch we'll get together, you and I."

Julie moved furniture, magazines, books, discarded lamps, the usual attic debris, and Mrs. Mott "wiped up" before she replaced them, her faded hair stringing out in straight clumps from her exertion. "Working together this way," she told Julie, "you can get a lot done."

But Julie slowed up when she came to the stack of canvases that had been Margaret Field's. She crouched on the floor and turned one after another to the light. The colors were so clear and vivid, the brushstrokes so bold and certain, that Julie loved to look at them. In comparison her own efforts always seemed fussy and unsure. "Not a bit like Margaret." The old guilt came back to haunt her.

But she shook off the memory. I'll never paint like mother anyway—because I'm a different sort of person. But I'll paint. I *know* that!

She turned a vivid still life of a bowl of zinnias toward the window. "Look, Mrs. Mott! Isn't this beautiful?"

The cleaning woman peered with watery eyes. "It's sure bright," she said. "Why don't you hang it up downstairs? That livin' room could stand some color."

Julie considered the suggestion. She wondered if her father would mind. Somehow, by unspoken agreement, they had never hung any of Margaret's paintings around. They were too alive, too definitely hers. They made them both remember too much. But now, after all these years, the memory had dimmed so much for Julie that the paintings regained their identity, their separateness. She lifted the framed canvas into her arms.

Downstairs, on the narrow mantel above the blocked-up living room fireplace, the brilliant zinnias shone out with a radiance that made the rest of the room drab. But Julie left the painting there nevertheless. To have returned it to the attic darkness would have seemed too mean a thing to do.

Nobody used the living room much in the winter anyway. It was too cold and lifeless. The kitchen was the hub of the house. In fact it was a month later, on the first day of March, when the last snow was melting and the air had turned freakishly springlike, that Julie again opened the door.

She was ushering in Miss Farrell whose promised visit was unexpected when it came and she was very ill at ease.

There was a daintiness about Miss Farrell that seemed out of place at the farm. The minute the teacher stepped from her little black sports car Julie sensed it. She wore high heels, for one thing, and her dark suit was as urban as the neatness of her hair. Julie had been sprawled on the stoop with Sonny when the car drove up, her right hand buried deep in the dog's ruff, which had grown long and thick over the winter. There was no time to duck into the house to comb her hair or wash up. She was caught.

But Miss Farrell seemed not to notice her pupil's appearance. She called a greeting to Julie as she opened the yard gate and then said, "Oh, what a beautiful collie!" as Sonny stretched and stood up.

Julie looked down at the dog affectionately, ready to agree, but Miss Farrell hurried on. "Don't tell me he's one of the puppies you used to sketch?"

Julie nodded. "He's nearly a year old now." Then she remembered her manners. "Won't you come in?"

As always when a stranger came to the farm, the house looked especially dingy. Paint was peeling from the walls of the narrow hall, and one of the stair rails was leaning. She couldn't take Miss Farrell into the kitchen—she just couldn't—it wouldn't seem right. That was how she came to open the living room door.

The first thing she saw—and the art teacher saw, too—was the painting of the zinnias. It glowed on the mantel in shocking contrast to the yellowed wallpaper behind it, increasing the ugliness of the room.

"Julie, how perfectly lovely!" Miss Farrell stood still, looking at the picture.

"Mother painted it," Julie murmured, following her gaze.

Then, with unaffected interest, Miss Farrell's eyes began to slide around the room. "And what a fine old house!" she said, surprisingly. "With those cupboards, and the deep windowsills, what a charming room this could be!"

She walked quickly across the floor and tapped with her knuckles below the mantel, listening. "Of course, there's a fireplace here." She tapped on the right, then moved several feet to the left. "A big one. Listen."

She caught Julie's eye and laughed apologetically. "I've been forgetting myself, my dear. Old houses are my passion."

But Julie was intrigued, not offended. "You mean—you think—something could be done with this room?" She looked helplessly around.

Miss Farrell seemed embarrassed, as though she felt she had over-stepped her bounds. Julie, however, pressed her. "It's so ugly. If you could help me—"

"It isn't ugly, Julie. The room has fine proportions. But I have no real right to make suggestions. It's just that if it were mine—"

"What would you do if it were yours?" Julie prodded as the teacher hesitated again.

"I'd scrape off the wallpaper and paint the walls and woodwork all one color—a pale, pale yellow or a pinky tan, I think. I'd see if you couldn't persuade your dad to open up the fireplace. It wouldn't be hard. I'd take down the shades—they keep out too much light—and hang crisp white curtains at the windows." Julie could see that Miss Farrell couldn't stifle her enthusiasm. "Aside from the fireplace job you could do all the work yourself."

"This summer," Julie agreed dreamily.

"This summer? What's going on this summer?" Tom Ferguson stamped into the room. Then, in one glance, he saw the painting of the zinnias and Linda Farrell. He stopped abruptly, confused for a second. Miss Farrell walked forward and held out her hand.

"I'm afraid I've been putting ideas into your daughter's head, Mr. Ferguson. Forgive me. I can't seem to resist an urge to restore old houses, and this is such a fascinating one." She smiled apologetically. "But I've been talking out of turn. Maybe I should have made restoration my business instead of teaching art."

Tom, instead of taking offense, looked around him curiously. "What kind of ideas?"

"I was thinking it would be fun to open up that fireplace."

Julie watched her father walk over and tap on the wall much as

Miss Farrell had done. "Might at that." She shot her teacher the glance of an ally and nodded, beaming.

"Could we, Dad, d'you think?"

"Might," Tom repeated. Then he turned to Miss Farrell, dismissing Julie. "You had somethin' you wanted to talk to me about?"

Julie answered the signal to leave, and walked down to the meadow with Sonny. She knew, without being there, that the teacher would be telling her dad that she, Julie, might do well at art school. Miss Farrell, along with other members of the faculty, were making it their business to call on parents of their most promising pupils this spring. It neither surprised Julie nor excited her particularly. She'd been planning to go to art school all along.

But the impact of the conversation with Miss Farrell on Julie's father *was* surprising. He brought up the subject at supper, and seemed to look at Julie through new eyes, as though he were almost impressed.

"That young teacher of yours thinks you should go to art school. Says you've got talent." He paused, then continued, "Like your mother, maybe."

Julie nodded, astonishingly sure of herself. "I've always sort of counted on going to the Academy, Dad. If we can afford it, when I get through high school."

Her father stared beyond her. "We'll make it our business to afford it," he said.

He sat a minute, his dessert plate pushed back, puffing at his pipe. "She says you did some sketches of the pups awhile back. I'd like to see 'em if you've still got 'em around."

Julie kept her voice level but her heart was thumping with pleasure that her dad should at last be interested. "They're still upstairs. They're not much, really, but I'll get them if you like."

She didn't bring her mother's portfolio down. She brought just the sketches, in her hand, and put them down on the table before her dad. Tom turned them over thoughtfully, considering each one. Occasionally a bit of action, some puppy foolishness, would make him grin. Then he would nod and say, "Not bad."

It was high praise and Julie knew it. She leaned against his chair and looked over his shoulder until he was through. Then she walked around to her place and suddenly, unaccountably, she found herself telling her father about the trip to the publisher's. "I know now how silly it was, but I wanted to keep Sonny so much!"

The dog, lying on the rag rug by the door, got up and crossed the kitchen to Julie's chair at the sound of his name. He held up a paw and made a friendly noise in his throat, asking for her attention.

Julie dropped a hand on his head, smoothing the short hair around his eyes. Then her hand halted and stiffened as her father said:

"That reminds me. I had a letter from Lonsdale today."

Julie didn't move. The hand on the dog's head scarcely trembled, although her entire arm was tense. Her eyes, looking directly into her father's, were very grave.

"Yes?"

Tom was fumbling in his pocket. "I've got it here somewhere." He ran his hands into every pocket in turn, while Julie waited without expression.

"Well, anyway, he's not planning to enter him in the spring shows. He thinks he'd rather hold him till fall." Tom gave up the search. "That was the gist of the thing."

His meaning wasn't quite clear to Julie. "Hold him till fall?" Did that mean he'd be coming for Sonny soon?

Tom nodded. "He wants to wait until he gets his full growth," he added, still not answering Julie's unspoken question.

"Does that mean—?" Julie couldn't say it.

Finally her father caught on. "That means Sonny'll stay with us until Mr. Lonsdale's ready to start grooming him," he said gruffly.

Julie relaxed all over. She sighed without knowing it. The hand on Sonny's muzzle started to stroke the hair back toward his ears again. But she tried to keep the relief out of her voice when she said, "That's nice."

Julie had a birthday party for Sonny. It was a kid thing to do, and she wouldn't have admitted it to anyone, but on the day he was a year old she bought him a composition bone, and together they walked up the brook to her "place," which she had not revisited since last summer.

Sonny accepted the gift with dignified graciousness, taking the bone daintily in his white teeth and laying it on the ground so that he might sniff it. The smell of Julie was around it, and he liked that, so he took it between his forepaws and nibbled at it.

"You even know how to say thank you," Julie told him, pleased.

Sonny, in his second spring, was even more beautiful than the remembered Scarlet. He had all of her grace, her cleanness of line, her obvious breeding, but he had something else besides. Beneath the noble bearing that was so like his mother's, Sonny had a bone structure that was as strong as it was solid. He loved to run for the sheer joy of motion, and he had a mile-eating stride that Tom said was inherited from his wolf ancestors.

Julie was as conscious as her father of the collie's soundness of movement, of his straight front legs, his good spring of rib, the rippling beauty of his muscles in action. But it was something beyond even this that she felt was his greatest attribute. Sonny was the most intelligent dog she had ever known.

From earliest puppyhood Sonny had learned to react to her voice in all its phases, to read from experience its many shades of meaning. He understood, from constant hearing, many simple words and phrases of command, disapproval, or praise. A scowl would bring him to Julie with a rush, to rub his nose comfortingly against the back of his mistress's hand. He would wag his tail in joyous excitement when Julie laughed. And when he realized from her tone that he had done something to make Julie especially proud of him, he would catch her hand between his jaws in simulated savageness, pretending to bite it ferociously although he exerted no pressure at all.

As Sonny grew older, Julie could almost feel the bond between them strengthen. It frightened her a little, that Sonny seemed to be able to see past mere facial expression and to read her varying moods. He was so intensely her dog that it was hard to think of him as a loan, although she had long been reconciled to what she must do.

Sometimes she almost wished that Mr. Lonsdale would come for him now, get the parting over and done with, instead of leaving him for a second summer at the farm. But then she scolded herself—that's selfish!—because the freedom of the life at Deepdale was doing Sonny so much good, was creating the very qualities a champion show dog should have.

"Country-bred—you can always tell 'em," Julie had heard her father say when he was admiring an especially fine dog. She wanted Sonny to have everything—everything! She wanted him to be the best.

Julie remembered a remark her English teacher had once made. "'Best' is a word never used in advertising. It's a boasting sort of word, rarely true. Handle it cautiously when you write." But that is what Julie wanted Sonny to be. Best! Best of class, best of breed, best of show. She dreamed great dreams for him to stifle the dull ache in her heart.

She also did something else, more sensible. She threw herself into a number of projects, at school and at home, with an enthusuasim that she had never shown before.

Winning the poster contest had done something for Julie. She wasn't afraid anymore. She still had moments of agonizing shyness, but she was no longer frightened that the girls might consider her odd or plain or stupid. She did her best to conform to the accepted pattern of behavior, but she couldn't help, from there on, what they thought of her, and she didn't really very much care. The knowledge that she would leave Meadowbrook High in two years and go on to the Academy was bound up in this. She was Julie Ferguson, and she recognized her emerging personality for the first time. She also understood dimly that this very readiness to be herself was the same quality she had always admired in Connie Blake. Anne didn't have it. Anne was a nice girl, a pretty girl, a popular girl, but she was a sheep. Julie no longer yearned to be like Anne.

Once this train of thought had been carried to its conclusion, Julie stopped thinking about herself. She became part of the general busy-ness that always signalized the spring term, and she kept herself from rushing home each afternoon to be with Sonny by a creditable effort of will.

A dozen things helped her. She discovered an urge to participate in spring sports. Miss Farrell persuaded her to mount and mat a group of her puppy sketches for an annual art exhibition. The sophomores all became acutely conscious that next year they would be juniors, and they held a series of class meetings preceding the examination period which were marked by a new seriousness.

At one of these meetings class officers were nominated and Julie unaccountably found herself on her feet suggesting Connie Blake's name for the vice-presidency. Once thus committed, she felt compelled to carry her nomination through with some mild campaigning, and when Connie was finally elected she was as delighted as though she had received the post herself.

Connie thanked her warmly when Julie offered her congratulations. "I don't know why you've been so nice to me."

"It wasn't being nice," Julie told her. "I just felt sure you'd be the right person for the job."

That very same day, when the junior-class officers were posted on the bulletin board, Julie had a pleasant surprise. Marcia Redding, in gym clothes, passed her on the way to the athletic field, from which Julie and her class were returning. She smiled, spoke, then turned and called, "Oh, Julie!"

Julie stopped while Marcia walked back, proud to be seen standing with this important senior in the main school yard.

"*Blade's* electing its new staff, and your name was one of three brought up for art editor. I'm supposed to see if you'd accept it."

"Accept it!" Julie was overwhelmed.

"It doesn't mean you're elected," Marcia told her bluntly. "Just nominated. As a matter of fact you've never done any drawing for *Blade* and one of the other nominees has. Why don't you get busy and turn in a cover design, or a few cartoons?"

Julie hesitated. "Don't you think that would look awfully—pushy? As though I were falling over myself to get the job?"

"What if it does?" Marcia shrugged. "That's the way jobs are gotten, you know."

Julie had never thought of that. Unlacing her gym shoes on the bench that ran along between the walls of lockers, she kept wondering if Marcia Redding had worked hard to get her job on *Blade*. It scarcely seemed possible. People like Marcia, and the football captain, and the senior-class president, always seemed to have honors fall into their laps. Could it be any other way?

Marcia said it was, and Julie respected Marcia.

Well, if working would get her places, Julie could work. It was worth a determined try.

A week later she approached the *Blade* office timidly with three cartoons. The little room was tucked under the back stairs to the auditorium stage, and she had never been in it before. It seemed glamorous to her now, in the way a newspaper office is glamorous—untidy, creative, smelling faintly of paper and ink. She'd like to be a part of the crowd that worked here.

There was no one at either of the two desks, however, when Julie pushed open the door. She dumped the cartoons, signed in the lower right-hand corner with her name, on the nearest of the desks, and ran. Then the waiting began.

Life, Julie had long since decided, is mostly waiting. Waiting to grow up. Waiting to go to the Academy. Waiting to say farewell to Sonny. Waiting to know the result of the poster contest. And now waiting for this.

But it is possible, she was discovering, to become philosophical even about waiting. It was less desperate a time now than it had been when she was waiting to find out about her *Pinafore* poster. If she should be elected to *Blade* she would be thrilled, but if another art editor were chosen her life would not stop completely.

To divert her attention she began to consider in some detail the redecoration of the living room, and one afternoon after high school she sought out Miss Farrell.

The art teacher was cleaning out the cupboards in the art classroom. Her face was smudged with blue chalk and damp tendrils of hair clung to her forehead, making her seem younger to Julie than ever before. She looked up with a welcoming smile.

"Hello, Julie. Come on in."

"Will I be interrupting?"

"I'll welcome an interruption. This is a disheartening job."

Julie went into the room and closed the door behind her. She glanced down at a handful of paint advertisements she carried and came right to the point. "I want to do over the living room, the way you suggested, but I don't quite know where to begin."

Miss Farrell's smile broadened to a grin. "I don't wonder." Then she turned suddenly serious. "It'll be a big job, Julie. Have you lots of patience?"

Julie grinned in return. "Not lots. But maybe it'll teach me some."

Miss Farrell came over and sat down on one of the long tables, kicking a chair into a comfortable position for her feet. "You've got some color charts there?"

Julie held out the folders. "I'm such a babe in arms that I don't even know what type of paint to use—oil base or latex."

Miss Farrell considered. "If your plaster's in good condition, I'd use an oil base paint with a dull finish," she said thoughtfully. "It will cost a little more than latex, but it will give you a more lasting job."

Busily, they began to plan. First of all, Miss Farrell explained, Julie should wet the old wallpaper and scrape it off. This would be a long and laborious job, one best not tackled until school had closed. Meanwhile, however, she could buy the paint—two gallons of it—and store it until she was ready to put it on the walls.

It was on a day soon after she bought the paint that the graduation issue of *Blade* came out. Two of Julie's cartoons were published, and they had a wistful as well as a humorous quality that gave them double appeal. They were concerned with a leggy freshman, ill-adjusted and shy. When Miss Farrell saw them she laughed.

"Whom were you poking fun at, Julie? These have a *barb*."

Julie was surprised to find herself answering, with unembarrassed honesty, "Myself."

In the same issue the new staff of *Blade* was announced, and Julie saw her own name jump away from the page to meet her. She kept turning back to reread the item, relishing the look of "Julie Ferguson" in print.

The girls all gathered around after school to add their congratulations to Miss Farrell's, and Anne said, "Want to catch the late bus and walk down to the drugstore for a Coke?" Julie agreed happily. Her cup of good fortune was very nearly full.

When June heralded the close of school, Julie said good-bye to her classmates with real regret. "Come see me," she urged each of the girls, as she never would have dared the summer before. "It isn't much of a bike ride. Just two miles."

The very first week of vacation Julie stripped the living room of all movable furniture, covered the rest in old sheets, and began the job of peeling the brittle paper off the walls. Her dad didn't offer to help; he was up to his ears in harvesting his crop of alfalfa and came in at night too dead tired to take an interest in Julie's ambitious project. Timidly, one evening, she reminded him of his agreement to open up the fireplace. She knew she was exaggerating, that it hadn't exactly been an agreement, but she thought putting it that way would carry more weight.

She was mistaken. Tom brushed the suggestion aside with: "Don't pester me, Julie. You know this is my busy season. I haven't got time for any inside work at all."

Julie was disappointed. Charged with energy, she would have liked to work on the redecoration of the living room to the exclusion of everything else. She tried to take comfort in the fact that her father hadn't said a direct no, but it was hard to be patient—terribly hard.

Dick, who was again working part-time at the farm, stopped in occasionally to see how she was getting on. Usually he found Julie on a stepladder, streaked with dirt and perspiration, attacking some particularly clinging section of paper with vicious concentration.

Because she was so busy she didn't have time to dwell on Dick or worry about her effect on him, and as a result their old friendship seemed to reawaken. She even began to ask his advice.

"If you were me, what would you do about this woodwork?"

Dick ran a hand over one of the windowsills thoughtfully. "Sand it down."

"Sand—what d'you mean?" Julie's knowledge of such terminology was decidedly vague.

Dick didn't mind. It made him feel important to be able to explain. "Sandpaper, Peanut, is an old American institution. You buy medium grade, at the hardware store, and rub it. Like this. Presto! A smooth surface for your new paint."

"Did you say 'presto'?" Julie was at least experienced enough to know that nothing happened quickly in this business.

"Well, maybe not presto," Dick conceded. "But it wouldn't take you more than a couple of days' steady work."

He dropped in again a week later, when the walls were completely scraped and the sanding was well under way.

"I hate you heartily, Dick Webster," Julie told him. "You're the guy that got me into this. If it hadn't been for you I'd have slapped the new paint right on regardless. And now look at me!" But the smile in her eyes contradicted the tone of her voice. Dick only chuckled.

He stayed around, leaning on the sheet-covered sofa, and talked to her for half an hour. He seemed fidgety, which wasn't like Dick, and Julie began to sense that he had something on his mind. Finally he blurted it out.

"D'you remember John Ford?"

Julie stopped rubbing and thought back.

"A cousin of mine. He came to visit us the first summer you lived here."

"Oh, *Tubby!*" A picture of Tubby Ford struggled up through Julie's swampy memory to the surface. A fat boy, older than either she or Dick, his voice changing, already talking about girls in a way that had seemed sissy at the time.

"He's coming again, for the weekend," Dick said, rubbing one leg against the other, avoiding Julie's eyes.

"Oh." Julie didn't know what was expected of her. She looked curiously at Dick.

"I was thinking, Dick blurted out, "I ought to get him something to do."

112

Julie nodded, understanding now, sympathetic. "I know. There isn't much around here. Except swimming."

"I mean Saturday night." Dick spilled it with a rush. "I was thinking maybe we could pick up Connie in town and all go to the movies."

The sandpaper, wrapped around a thick board, dropped to Julie's side. She tried to cover her surprise unsuccessfully.

"You mean—all of us?"

Dick, now that the proposition was stated, recovered his assurance. "You and Connie and Tubby and me."

A date. Dick was asking her to go on a double date! Julie couldn't figure out quite whose date she was to be, Dick's or Tubby's, though she suspected the latter. But that didn't matter, really. The four of them would all be together. A double date with Connie Blake, one of the most popular girls in the sophomore—junior! she corrected herself—class.

"Why," she told Dick, trying to sound casual, "I think that would be fun."

"Okay, then. I'll be getting in touch with you." Dick, his business transacted, made a hasty exit. Julie turned back to her sandpapering, but once she heard the front door slam behind him she sank weakly to the floor, her back against the wall.

Like all important things, things to which she had given a disproportionate amount of thought, the actual incident seemed trivial. She had wondered so often who it would be, what he would say, what she would say, when she was asked for her first date. She'd thought of it as rather different, somehow. It seemed a little cut-and-dried—Dick having a friend for the weekend, and wanting to fix up a foursome for the movies.

But then she shook herself. What was she kicking about? It was better this way, far better, than having to go out with a boy alone. Particularly a boy who wasn't Dick. Julie had learned the rules from young women's magazines. Go out with a boy you know, go with a crowd, and *do* something. That was the way to scare off the jitters. All the advice was the same.

She wondered if she should ask her father. It seemed too silly to say, "Dad, can I go to the movies Saturday night with Dick and his cousin and Connie Blake?" He'd just grunt and wrinkle his forehead and say: "Sure. Sure. Of course." He was indifferent to anything but work these days.

Finally she put it, not as a question, but as a statement. "Dick's cousin is here for the weekend. He's driving us in town to the movies." But she finished weakly. "Is that all right?"

Tom grunted, just as she had expected him to, his mind a mile away, but then the words seemed to act like a boomerang and shock him into alertness. "Huh? Who? Where?"

Julie repeated.

"Who's driving?"

"This cousin of Dick's—John Ford." She used the "John" because it made the boy seem older, but actually she could only remember him as Tubby, with dimples in his elbows and a deep cleft in his chin. "We're picking up Connie Blake," she added with what she hoped was sophistication, "on our way."

The fact that his daughter had a date seemed to smack Tom across the face. He felt inadequate to the situation, and Julie could sense it. "Before you go," he said, drawing his eyebrows together, "I want to meet this boy."

Julie was half embarrassed, half amused. "Okay, Dad," she answered, and since she had Sonny's dinner in her hands she went on up to the barn. She whistled, and Sonny came flying around the edge of the building at once. He leaped against her playfully and Julie cried: "Down, boy! You'll knock me over!" Then, for a second, she stooped and cuddled him. Tom, from the yard gate, watched the pair, Julie with her breeze-tossed hair almost the color of Sonny's coat.

114

Julie put her arms over her head and wriggled into her dress. It was a new dress, this summer. She had bought it herself, at the Corner Shop, sternly refusing to be tempted by the pinks and blues she loved, and remembering Mrs. Sawyer's advice. Made of linenlike fabric, the dress was an amber color that exactly matched her hair.

Standing in front of the mirror, Julie cocked her head critically. Maybe she looked too all-one-color, with her skin tanned to the same shade as the dress. Only her eyes were different—dark. She wondered if she had been wise after all.

Opening one of the top bureau drawers, she took out her brush and started to brush her hair, sweeping down with a long stroke and then holding the brush at the end of the shoulder-length strands so that the hair fell slowly from it, glistening in the pink afterglow of the setting sun. She was wearing it almost straight again, pulled back sharply from her heart-shaped face, having given up the impossible attempt to copy Marcia Redding's curly hairdo. She felt that it was plain but comfortable. Perhaps too plain—tonight.

She didn't want to look like a little girl. She wanted to look old. Older! It was a burning ambition suddenly, but she didn't know how to accomplish it. She sighed.

Dick would be coming soon—and Tubby Ford. Julie tried to imagine what Tubby might now be like and she had a cold stab of doubt. Fatter than ever? Ridiculously dimpled? A funny boy at whose jokes she would be expected to giggle and respond? Desperately she began to wish she'd never agreed to embark on this Saturday night venture. Why, why, why had she ever imagined it might be fun?

She walked over to the window and looked out on the slumbering farm. To stay here for the evening, basking in the glow of the flaming sun, walking up to the ridge with the collie, being alone—all these things seemed fantastically good. And the alternative—

Connie marching ahead with Dick, sure of herself, possessive, while Julie was left behind to hurry along with a toddling, puffing fat boy, who was growing in her mind like a genie emerging from smoke, incredible, grotesque. Connie knowing when to laugh, what to say, while Julie was speechless, embarrassed, miserable. The drugstore after the movies, and people coming in, the crowd looking over Julie Ferguson's date and turning away to hide their grins. Ridicule!

Julie's hands grasped the edge of the bureau and the mirror reflected the panic in her eyes. "Don't be absurd!" she commanded herself aloud. "You got yourself into this. You've got to go through with it." At the same moment she heard the rattle of the Webster car as it started to roll down the hill.

She didn't look out the window—she couldn't—as the brakes rasped on by the yard gate. She heard Dick's voice greet her father, who must have been sitting on the stoop, and she bit her lip impatiently because she thought it looked as though he were obviously waiting there. She heard Tom's rumbled response, and a stranger's voice, deeper than Dick's, saying a straightforward, "Good evening." She waited until her father shouted up the stairwell, "Julie!" then forced herself to walk sedately downstairs.

For a moment, as she went down the narrow hall and looked through the screen door to the porch, she thought she must be mistaken. This couldn't be Tubby Ford! Not this tall, lean, hard-muscled boy. Then, as Dick hastened to introduce her, the boy smiled, and there was the cleft in the chin, and a way his eyes had of twinkling, that stirred her memory.

"I'd never have known you!" she gasped.

Tubby laughed. "I've thinned out some."

"Some! He's taken off two hundred pounds!" said Dick.

"I remember," drawled Tom, "I was a fat *little* boy. Fat and short. I went through plenty of torture waiting to thin out."

Julie looked at her father in astonishment. Tom Ferguson self-conscious? She'd never have dreamed—

"It isn't much fun!" agreed Tubby.

They chatted for a few minutes, the four of them; then Dick became uneasy. "Well, shall we be going?" he asked.

Julie had another bad moment as she settled herself between the two boys on the front seat of the car. She had forgotten that she would be alone with them on the ride into Meadowbrook, that she'd have to make conversation.

But they were talking across her, above her head, rapidly, importantly. There didn't seem to be much that was necessary to say. Now and then Julie made murmurs in her throat signifying agreement, and once she asked a question, but most of the conversation was out of her hands.

Gradually she began to relax, lulled by her lack of immediate responsibility and the soothing motion of the car. She stole sidelong glances at Tubby—John, Dick called him now—and wondered that she had been concerned for her own possible position. The thing that worried her now was more natural to her—would she conceivably be equal to him?

Maybe when they got Connie . . . Pinning her hopes on Connie kept Julie from being too afraid.

The Blake porch, tented by flowering shrubs, looked wide, dark, and cool. Connie came out of the gloom in a white dress and greeted the three of them, putting out her hand boyishly when Dick introduced John.

"Shall we sit down or do you want to get right off?"

How does she know just the way to put things? Julie wondered. How does she know?

Dick was consulting his watch, and there was a little discussion about the probable time at which the movie began. Julie was sure that the others were wrong and that she really knew, but she didn't say so. Sometimes her shyness stood in her good stead.

They decided, finally, to leave at once, and it was still dusk when they entered the movie theater, passing under the lighted marquee. A small thrill crept up Julie's spine as she and Connie waited in the lobby for the boys to buy the tickets. She had enviously watched older girls stand this same way—so many times!

Connie whispered, "Where did Dick *ever* get hold of John? I think he's neat!"

Julie whispered back, "He's his cousin. He used to be fat. I was never so surprised."

There was a minor tangle over the seating, and Julie found herself between John and a stranger, with Connie and Dick, her anchors, on John's other side. The movie had already started, and they all fell silent, concentrating on catching up with the plot.

Afterward, when they emerged to the lighted, familiar street, the spell of the filmed drama still lingered, and the return to reality was a pull.

"How about a Coke?" suggested Dick, and John Ford looked at Julie and shook her arm playfully. "Come back, Julie. Come back."

Julie flushed and said, still dreamily: "That would be nice. I'm thirsty." Connie went on ahead with Dick, and she tagged along with John, as she had known she would.

But instead of feeling awkward, she felt proud and gay. She chattered to John about the movie as though she had known him—as indeed she had—for years. He was easy to talk to, somehow. He treated her with a sort of elder-brotherly, half-teasing solicitude that she found very pleasant and comfortable. When the four of them were seated, facing each other, in a booth at the drugstore, she expanded to such an extent that she felt almost witty. Her brown eyes, so solemn when she was not animated, began to glisten and shine.

John liked her. Julie could tell that. He talked to her as much as he talked to Connie, and his grin, when he caught her glance unexpectedly, was infectious. Afterward, Julie couldn't remember why they had all laughed so much, in the drugstore and later, on the way home. But it had been fun, that she knew. "Great fun!"

The next day it was arranged that they should all go swimming, up the brook, in the afternoon. Julie couldn't have told whether she invited everyone, or whether Connie had suggested it, or Dick. But she did remember saying: "You'll have to excuse the house. It's a wreck. I'm doing over the living room," and she caught the quick flicker of special interest in John Ford's eyes.

"I'm going to be an architect when I get out of school," he made a point of telling her.

The next day he insisted on being shown the stripped living room while Connie changed into her suit.

"Wow," he said admiringly. "You're doing a big job!"

Dick was standing behind her. "And is she slow!" he put in, truthfully. "Like molasses."

John was eying the blocked-up fireplace.

"I'm going to open that up," Julie told him. "I hope. When Dad has time."

"I wish I were going to be here next week," John said, sincerely. "I'd get a kick out of helping."

"Can't you stay?" The words were out before Julie thought.

John shook his head. "I've got a summer job, driving a delivery truck. I'd get fired."

"Besides, we couldn't feed him," added Dick. "He eats too much." He dodged the pass John made at him with neat agility as Connie came down the stairs.

Connie and Dick ran ahead up the brook to the dam, full of laughter and horseplay. Julie followed more slowly with John, answering one question after another about her plans for the living room.

"I'll bet you draw, too, don't you?" he said unexpectedly.

Julie looked surprised. "Yes. How did you know?"

He looked down. "Your hands."

Julie followed his glance, bending an elbow and holding a stubby, short-fingered hand out in front of her. "But—but my hands are so *homely*," she protested. "They're not artistic at all."

"Long-fingered, artistic hands are the bunk," John told her firmly. "I've never seen an artist yet with beautiful hands." He took her wrist and shook it gently. "You've got workmanlike hands. That's what you'll need."

Suddenly Julie found herself telling John all about her plans for art school. The assurance her dad had given her that she really would be able to go to the Academy meant something concrete to work toward, a future to plan for that gave her a new feeling of stability. She felt the same firmness of purpose in John. For he was going to Penn, he told her, to the School of Architecture there. Ever since he had been a

119

youngster, he confessed, he had wanted to do just this one thing. Julie nodded sympathetically. She understood.

The afternoon passed quickly—too quickly. The four of them swam and dove and played water tag, then lay in the sun and talked. Julie hated to say good-bye when they left.

"I really wish I could stay and help with that fireplace!" John shouted from the car. And Julie shouted back, "I wish you could, too."

Julie often repeated that wish as one summer week slipped into another and still Tom Ferguson labored on the multitude of outside jobs at the farm. Julie mentioned the fireplace to him once or twice, tentatively, because she fretted at being held up by this final task that must precede the painting of the room. Her father, however, was only irritated by the repetition.

"Stop heckling me, Julie," he finally shouted. "I'll get to it when I have time, and not before."

Julie wandered in and out of the house like a lost soul, fuming. She wondered if this choking impatience were just part of being young. She hoped so. It was awful. To divert herself she filled a sketchbook with new impressions of Sonny, and on several afternoons one or another of the girls rode out for a swim. But the job she had set her heart on finishing went uncompleted as July melted into August. Julie realized with distress that the end of vacation loomed only a month away.

One Saturday afternoon she was lying on the bank of the swimming hole with Sonny stretched out beside her when Dick unexpectedly joined her, dressed in his swimming trunks.

"Hello, Julie," he greeted her. "It was so stinking hot I thought you might be up here."

"The water's lukewarm," Julie told him lazily. "It's not much good."

But Dick dove in and paddled around for a while anyway, cooling his hot skin. Then he threw himself down on the bank beside Julie and shut his eyes. He yawned once, unmusically, said, "Wow, I'm sleepy," and in five minutes he was snoring softly, like a child.

Julie rolled over on her side, leaned on one elbow, and looked at him. She was swept for a second with the almost maternal emotion

120

she sometimes felt for Sonny. He seemed so defenseless, lying there—so young. Yet Dick awake no longer had this childlike, unguarded quality. His hard-muscled body was so tough, his deepening voice so direct, that he seemed closer to the man than the boy.

It was strange, Julie thought, that she should be surrounded by males, she who had always felt so desperately the need of a woman's tenderness and guidance. But then she lifted her chin, repenting her weakness. She wouldn't give up her men—Dad, Sonny, Dick—not for anything!

A fly tickled the boy's nose, and he stirred, frowning and grimacing. A swallow-tailed butterfly floated under the canopy of trees from the sunshine beyond and searched vainly for a flower. The water in the brook seemed idle, scarcely flowing. Time seemed to hesitate, breathless, and Julie had again the familiar sensation of waiting, half-expectant, half-agonizing, for she knew not what.

Sonny raised his head from his paws and searched Julie's face, sensing her disturbance. She pursed her lips in a soundless whistle and he moved over to her on cat feet, cuddling against her. In spite of the heat she circled his body with one bare arm and hugged him. Then all of a sudden her mood was broken and she got to her feet.

"I think I'd better be going home, Dick."

Dick's eyes flashed open and he stretched. "Okay." He sat up. "How about one more dip?"

"All right."

Dick went off the board, practicing his jackknife. Julie followed but she knew without asking that her dive no longer had the clean, polished form of the boy's. She dove again, resenting this, trying to make her body taut as a spring, but it was no good.

Dick climbed out, muddying the water by the bank, and Julie followed, accepting his help for a quick jerk upward. She shook out her hair over her wet shoulders and at once they walked toward home.

Before they reached the upper field a sharp whistle cut the air.

"That's Dad," Julie said. "He must want me."

Premonition, sharp as a knife, pierced her stomach as the whistle came again, and when she tried to whistle back her lips were dry and the sound she made was feeble and alarmed.

On the crest of the hill above the barn she stopped, staring, and

Dick hesitated, too, looking at her curiously, and then at the long car parked by the barn.

"He has come," Julie said tonelessly, "for Sonny."

She had a wild, immediate desire to throw her arms around Dick's neck, to cling to him, protesting, but she simply stood, expressionless, looking down. The wave broke over her and fell back as quickly as it had risen and she was drained and ready. She scarcely felt Dick take and squeeze her hand.

The collie was behind them, burrowing with forepaws and nose for the source of an interesting scent. Julie turned and called him. "Come on, boy!" When he reached her she crouched for an instant and buried her head in his neck. Then she walked quickly down toward the house, Sonny frolicking ahead.

Dick left her at the stable, to cut across the fields, and Julie said a level and controlled good-bye. She knew that the boy understood much of what this would mean to her, but she refused to admit his sympathy. The parting with Sonny was something she had faced that day in the springhouse. It was anticipated. Only for a moment had there been a shock. From now on Julie knew she could bear it alone.

The men, when she found them, were in the house. Mr. Lonsdale was standing in the hall, peering in through the living room door. When he saw Julie he greeted her and said, "Fine job you're doing here, my dear. This will make a charming room."

The praise tasted of ashes in Julie's mouth, but she managed to smile and thank him.

"You're planning to paint the walls?"

Julie nodded. "The walls and the woodwork will be the same color, a sort of pinky tan." She knew her father was watching her and she wanted no trace of emotion to be betrayed.

Mr. Lonsdale nodded in his turn. "The color of a woman's face powder."

Julie raised her eyebrows, surprised at his perception. "That's it."

Her father's laugh sounded overstressed. He made a half-hearted attempt at a joke, then stopped, his eyes on his daughter, who was facing Mr. Lonsdale.

"You've come for Sonny," she said.

It was a statement, not a question, and the breeder replied with another. "He's a mature dog now. I want to enter him in the fall shows."

"He has been up the brook with me. He'll need brushing before he leaves. Do you want me to see to it, Dad?"

The matter-of-factness of Julie's voice made the men relax. She sensed that they must have anticipated a traumatic leave-taking and were relieved that she was accepting it so coolly. As she went out to the stoop with the grooming brush she felt a sense of power surge through and around the deep-rooted sorrow that she was hiding. She was in command of her emotions. She could carry this off!

She was proud of herself, after Mr. Lonsdale left, in spite of the loneliness that was already creeping through her. It was right that Sonny should go. Born to a line of champions, to a great heritage, he was no dog that should live out his life on a farm. All her reason leaped to her aid, pushing the collie from her toward his destiny.

A show dog! A champion show dog—that's what Sonny should and would be. Julie made every effort to convince herself that when she saw his picture in the newspapers, when she read about him, heaped with one honor after another, it would make up for what she was feeling now. But she couldn't visualize Sonny in a dog-show ring, though she had been to several shows with her dad. She could see him only as she saw him last, standing, surprised, on the backseat of Mr. Lonsdale's car, his tulip ears cocked, his eyes questioning, and a series of sharp barks racketing from his throat.

Tom Ferguson, on the hot, still evening of Sonny's departure, dried the supper dishes for Julie.

"You needn't, Dad," Julie told him, embarrassed, but Tom insisted. It was a little thing that he could do.

Neither of them mentioned the dog, but Julie knew that her father, in a lesser way, shared her sense of loss. Silences fell between them that neither could fill. Conversation was forced, sporadic, though each of them was making a valiant fight for normality. The dishes finished, Tom stamped around the house on heavy feet, challenging the quiet. Finally he joined Julie, who was sitting on the porch steps.

"Want to drive in town and see a movie, kid?"

"I don't think so, thanks. You go."

Tom strode back into the house, slamming the screen door. Julie could feel him behind her, standing in the hallway, puffing at his eternal pipe. Then she heard him open the closed living room door.

Presently his voice boomed out. "Say, Julie!"

Julie, without turning, said, "Yes?"

"Come here a minute, will you?"

Julie got up and walked into the house.

"About this fireplace," Tom said gruffly, indicating the blocked chimney with a gesture of his pipe. "I was just thinking—the farm can take care of itself for a day now—we might get at this thing tomorrow morning. If you can tote plaster and clean up after me, I can do the heavy work."

"All right. Fine."

Julie's voice lacked the enthusiasm that it would have carried a day before, but she did her best to let her father know that she appreciated his gesture. She knew quite well that the peak of summer work had not yet dropped off, that only because of Sonny would the offer have been made. He was taking every available way of saying he was sorry, of trying to make up to her . . .

They opened the fireplace the next morning. It wasn't such a big job after all. Tom was back in the fields by noon, and Julie was left to clear up the last of the debris. She made herself a sandwich and carried it, with a glass of milk, from the kitchen to the living room, settling down on the draped couch and staring at the large black opening thoughtfully.

It made the most enormous difference in the room! It was a huge fireplace—stand-in size—with a crane on which an old iron pot still swung. A wood cupboard had also been hidden under a thin coating of plaster, its black brass hinges intact. Julie could scarcely wait to get on the first coat of paint. Color, she knew, would transform the room still further. The walls and woodwork would need two coats, maybe three. It would be a big job and she was glad of it. She wanted to work—work hard!

In the two weeks that followed she spent about six hours a day on the job. She painted neatly, precisely, her artist's instinct for perfection coming to the fore. Even the first coat marked a definite improvement. The room grew larger, more interesting. The melting together of walls and woodwork took away a spottiness that distracted the eye. Tom, even, was impressed.

"With the fireplace open, we can use this room winters," he suggested. "I'll have to get Dick busy chopping us some wood."

As Julie worked she imagined the room completed. Her curtains, of crisp white cotton, were already made, painstakingly hemmed by hand. She planned to move in the Boston rocker from the kitchen to put beside the fireplace, and she hoped that after harvesttime there might be enough extra money to buy a new slipcover for the couch. The upholstered chairs were ugly, but they would have to do, and the Victorian walnut secretary that had been her grandmother's would lend some dignity and height to the room. Only one thing was missing in her picture—Sonny stretched before the hearth.

125

When Julie started the second coat she closed the door after her at the end of each day and ordered her father not to peek. "I don't want you to see it again until it's finished," she told him, "until the floor is waxed, and the curtains are hung, and the furniture is back in place."

He obeyed her command unquestioningly, falling in with what he considered a game, hoping that gradually Julie would forget Sonny in her interest in this new project, and thus he was willing to cooperate to the fullest extent. But he never knew that each day, when she walked up to the main road for the mail, Julie was seeing a gold-and-white collie bounding ahead of her, vibrant and glad, and that she shut her eyes to dismiss the image, sternly trying to think of something else.

One day, in the mailbox, she found a card from the parcel service addressed to herself, announcing that a shipment awaited her call at the Meadowbrook station. She thought at first it might be a mistake, and showed it to her father. But Tom phoned and checked, and together they drove in for the parcel late that afternoon.

It was no small package; it was a crate, four feet by two and a half, and it took both Tom and the agent to heave it into the trunk of the Ford.

"What do you suppose?" asked Julie, excited.

"It's beyond me," Tom replied. "It looks something like a chair."

He drove home carefully, guarding the crate against bumps, but he was as anxious as Julie to pry the boards loose and unwrap the bulky object. Julie danced around impatiently, sliding her hand between the boards and picking at the paper fruitlessly.

It *was* a chair, a high-backed wing chair, covered in flowered chintz, in warm colors that melted and glowed. To the back was fastened an envelope, addressed to Julie, and inside it was Philip Lonsdale's card, across the back of which was scrawled, "For Julie— whose loving care has developed a great dog."

Julie kept her eyes lowered, pretending she couldn't stop looking at the chair. She ran her hands over the smooth chintz, and felt the beauty of the curving arms. She was overwhelmed that Mr. Lonsdale should have sent her such a handsome present, but at the same time she felt sad. The chair would be beautiful by the living room fireplace. It would "make" the room, as Mrs. Sawyer would say. But the chair wasn't living, breathing, animate. It wasn't Sonny.

She shook off the vain regret and handed the card to her dad, saying, "It was terribly sweet of him, wasn't it? He really shouldn't have—"

"He should, too," Tom Ferguson interrupted. "He's right. You *made* that dog." Then, self-conscious because of his admission, he started hauling the crate off toward the rear of the house.

Julie finished the living room three days before the start of the fall term. Mrs. Mott scrubbed down the wide boards of the floor when the painting was finished, and Julie waxed and polished them with patient zeal. Alone, she dragged a pair of knobby black log holders down from the attic. They were no things of beauty, but they made the fireplace usable. She stocked the wood cupboard and laid three logs across the metal stand for effect, then helped Mrs. Mott wash the small-paned windows, and hung the pressed curtains with housewifely pride.

The figured Wilton rug that had covered the floor looked all wrong, somehow, with the new paint, so she rolled it up and stored it in the attic, collecting rag rugs from all parts of the house to scatter around in its place. Finally the furniture was arranged to her satisfaction, the beautiful wing chair in place. Its colors blended into the warm beige of the walls, and seemed to bring out the grain of the walnut in the old secretary. Behind the glass doors Julie arranged books—her mother's art books, her father's volumes on farming and animal husbandry, and finally the two gift books from Mr. Lonsdale, bright in their paper jackets. Except that it had, as yet, no "lived in" look, Julie felt that the room was complete.

Tom was away for the day, having driven to Philadelphia on some farm business, and Julie couldn't wait to display her handiwork. She called Connie and persuaded her to come out on her bike. "I still haven't got anything on the mantel and I need your help," she urged.

Connie didn't need much persuasion. She arrived around two o'clock and was satisfactorily ecstatic over Julie's color scheme and effect.

"It looks like something out of *House and Garden*," she sighed, sinking into the wing chair. "Honestly, it does!"

Julie protested. She knew that Connie was overcomplimentary. But in her heart she was delighted with the room. Never again would she have to apologize when she asked anyone into the house. "But what would you do with the mantel?" she asked finally. "It needs ornaments—a clock or something."

"Have you got a clock?" Connie was always practical.

"No."

Connie considered. "Candlesticks?"

Julie shook her head.

"Let's go rooting in the attic, then," Connie suggested. "I love attics."

It seemed to Julie that there wasn't much to root for in their particular attic, but Connie found an ironstone soup tureen which she carried downstairs with conviction. "It'll be perfect for flowers," she said.

Connie had picked some zinnias in her own garden and had brought them out with her. "As a housewarming present," she said.

"We still haven't got anything for the mantel," argued Julie.

But while she was rummaging in the top of the kitchen cabinet something turned up.

"What's that stack of plates?" Connie asked.

"These? Some old ones of Mother's, I guess. They're hard to eat off of—bumpy—we never use them."

"Bumpy?" Connie sounded puzzled. "Let's see."

Julie blew the dust from the top one and handed it down.

"Oh, I see." Connie laughed. "The design on them's raised. Pretty color, though. How many have you got?"

Julie counted. "Five. Two are alike and the rest are all different."

"We might try these on the mantel," said Connie reflectively, holding the plate away from her.

Julie snorted. "Those old things!" But she picked up another. "They are sort of quaint, I guess. There's a name for this kind of pottery, isn't there? It always reminds me of 'merry-go-round.'"

Connie thought. "Like 'carousel'? Majolica?"

"That's right! How did you know?"

"Mother loves old china and glass. She's always buying the stuff. I hear her talking." Connie, as she spoke, was washing the dishes under the tap. Their colors came up unclouded, subtle and luminous under the glaze.

Arranged on the narrow mantel in a prim, spaced row, Julie had to admit that they gave the room an air. "I'd never have thought of them, but I like them a lot," she said.

Connie put her vase of zinnias on the open secretary, and together the girls hung Margaret Field's painting of the same brilliant flowers on the opposite wall of the room.

"There!" Connie said. "Isn't everything lovely!"

Julie nodded. "You did the finishing touches. Somewhere along the line my imagination just stopped."

"I've picked up a lot of ideas from Mother," Connie said, deprecating her talents. "It's different for you, with only a man around." She hesitated, disconcerted.

Julie smiled, though a bit sadly. "That's right. It's hard sometimes without—a woman in the house." Then, afraid she sounded sorry for herself, she lightened her meaning with, "It's—oh, never knowing if you look right when you're going to a party."

But Connie was unafraid of sentiment, now that she was sure she hadn't hurt Julie's feelings. She lay back on the couch, her hands under her head for a pillow, and said: "It must be more than that even. Your dad's a lamb and all that, but I can't imagine him giving you any little tips, like Mother does us, on things like—well, how to act with boys, and how to have fun, and stuff."

Julie looked genuinely surprised. "Your mother does—that?"

Connie wagged her head. "Sure."

"What does she say?"

"Oh, I don't know. Well, one thing she said, a long time ago, when I was still in grammar school, was this: 'Never go to a party without taking something to it.' She has a theory that too many girls just go hoping they'll have a good time without ever thinking about giving somebody else a good time. I guess she's right, too."

Julie remembered Connie at the Freshman Frolic, dancing with Billy Bowen, and Dick's remark about her: "Y'know, that Blake gal's got something. Look at her making little Billy Brown think he's six foot two." Maybe that was how one got to be popular, making sure the other fellow had fun. Julie had never thought of that. She looked at Connie curiously. "But I always feel so *dumb*!"

Connie giggled. "So do I, lots of times. I guess all girls do."

Julie settled down on the floor, cross-legged, and held on to the toes of her sneakers with her hands. "You *really* think so?"

"Sure."

Julie considered. "Even Anne?"

Connie lifted her chin and laughed heartily. "Well, I don't know about Anne."

"Do you ever have trouble—*talking* to boys?"

"I used to. I used to try too hard. Try to be clever, say smart things. Boys don't like that."

"What do they like?" Julie probed.

Connie shrugged. "They like to be listened to, and they like you to laugh. If you're self-conscious they feel awkward, somehow." She was trying hard to put what she felt into words, and her face was puckered with concentration.

Julie nodded, understanding. "Gee, Connie, you know a lot," she breathed.

Connie sat up, suddenly embarrassed. "Me? I don't know a thing. Why, everybody in our crowd knows you're twice as bright as I am." She stood up. "Say! It's getting awfully late. I've got to be getting home."

There it was again. "Our" crowd. After Connie had pushed her bike up the sharp grade to the ridge, Julie sat down on the front steps and looked after her. Suppose—just suppose, that Connie was right—that her own sense of inadequacy was largely in her own head. Wouldn't that mean that just learning to forget herself would be the way out?

Julie didn't put these thoughts into words, but they floated around, interweaving and shadowy, in her searching mind. She sat on the steps until her dad chugged down the hill, and then took him inside and showed him her beautiful room.

They sat in the living room that night, Julie and her father. Both felt a little stiff and formal, as though they were out visiting. It would take time before they would be able to relax amid this unaccustomed elegance.

Tom read a farm bulletin, and glanced up, from time to time, to stare about him in wonder. Once Julie caught his eye, and he smiled at her and said, "Your mother would have liked this."

Julie sat in the wing chair with a mystery Dick had lent her, but she couldn't concentrate on the extravagances of the plot. She had to let the color and the newness of the room sink into her bones, become part of her, so that she could belong to it as she belonged to the kitchen and to her own unchanged bedroom.

Tom let the government bulletin lie on his knees as he lighted his pipe. "You know," he said, nodding his head toward his right elbow, "we could use a small table right here." He tossed a burnt match into the fireplace. "I could make one, maybe, if I could get some decent wood."

He stretched out his long legs and stared at his boots as he smoked—the old, familiar pose. Julie thought, as she watched him, that there seemed to be a slight edge to his contentment, as though it were not quite complete. Finally he spoke again.

"I've been thinking lately," he said without looking at Julie, "we could buy a dog, maybe. When Lonsdale gets a new litter, he'd likely sell us one of his puppies cheap."

Julie didn't look up either. She kept her eyes glued to the blurring lines of type in her book. But she shook her head vigorously and muttered, "I don't want a new dog, Dad. It wouldn't be the same."

It's a good thing, she thought as she undressed for bed that night, that school starts on Monday. It'll give me something to think about, something to do. For the first time, she realized with a start, she would really welcome the opening of school for its own sake. She was eager to see the girls again, eager to be a junior, eager to get busy on her job for *Blade*.

I'll wear my amber dress, she thought, as she fell asleep.

Monday was sparkling. Warm, sunny, with just a hint in the air of fall's coming excitement. Julie's anticipation lasted as she walked up the hill, early for the bus. All the other returning students looked as polished and fresh as she. There must have been an orgy of bath taking and hair washing last night, she laughed to herself. Even the high school, when she reached it, looked spruced up and shining, with only a trace of last term's stuffy smell lingering in the corners.

The bus was early, and Julie had time to go first of all to the art classroom, where Miss Farrell, as tanned as her pupil from the summer sunshine, was checking supplies.

"I had to come tell you how beautifully the living room turned out," Julie said at once. "At least I think it's nice. And it's really all due to you."

Miss Farrell waved a hand in protest. "It's not due to me at all, but I'm delighted to hear about it. Tell me what the fireplace was like when you opened it up."

Julie described the fireplace, and the cupboards beside it, drawing the proportions in the air with her hands.

"I can't wait to see it!" the art teacher exclaimed, her eyes full of interest. "I'm going to drive out some afternoon next week. That is, if I may?

"I was going to ask you to come," Julie replied.

She felt aglow with warmth and accomplishment as she stepped back into the corridor, where the usual first-day-back scramble was taking place, with nobody seeming to know just what to do or where to go. The voices of the junior girls she met sounded shrill and excited, those of the boys strangely deep. Freshmen scurried through the halls like frightened rabbits, popeyed and incredibly young. Julie felt superior but intensely sympathetic, and she answered their occasional questions with her very best smile.

When she reached her new homeroom, all the girls were there. Anne was tanned and glamorous from a month at the shore. Sue Downs was thinner. "I've been dieting—but dieting!" she confessed, rolling her eyes. Sidney was as overpowering and militant as ever. She scarcely favored Julie with a second glance, but this year Julie didn't really mind. Shirley Graham, in contrast, was gushing. "Julie!" she screamed, running up to her. "Connie's been telling me the most wonderful things about your house!" It was all very confusing but somehow familiar, and Julie grinned a lot and tried to be cordial to everyone, remembering Connie's advice.

Talk buzzed around Julie's head like the come-and-go droning of flies.

"Third-year French . . . practically all conversation . . . it's going to be awful!"

"Certainly you're going out for hockey. Everybody is. Julie's going to try for wing, aren't you, Julie?"

". . . the Junior Jamboree's to be early this year. Mr. Stewart told me so himself."

"I've never heard you say, Julie, are you going on to college?"

"I'm going to the Academy of Fine Arts," Julie heard her own voice saying proudly. "That's where my mother went." She settled herself and got into the conversation, which turned to required courses for art school and for college. Everybody's problem was different, and they all compared notes.

Anne said, "But I don't know *what* I want to do after I get out of high school." She looked around at the other girls, big-eyed and helpless, and Julie felt shocked and sorry for her until she realized with a start that Anne thought this attitude was cute.

Not to have a plan, not to have a passionate urge to do some one thing, not to have the deep-rooted desire to work and achieve—this beyond anything else seemed appalling to Julie. She turned her eyes away from Anne's so that she wouldn't betray her contempt, and watched Miss Durham, their new homeroom teacher, who had just come in from the main office and was trying to get her lists and schedules organized.

133

Gordon Wyatt, passing the desk where Julie sat, raised a finger in greeting. "Have a nice summer?"

Julie swung her legs around so that she faced the boy, genuinely glad to see him. "Grand!" She glanced at his tanned arms. "You been to camp?"

The tall boy shook his head. "Nope. Working on a farm up-country."

Julie raised her eyebrows, surprised. "Like it?"

"Sure. Except getting up at the crack of dawn."

Julie laughed. "That's what gets Dick." Then, afraid she might have sounded possessive, she hastened to explain. "Dick Webster, I mean. He works for Dad, summers. Helps with the stock and stuff."

Gordon was still as serious as ever. "You learn a lot that way," he said.

Julie's eyes followed him when he walked on. He had filled out since spring; he seemed older, huskier. Some of the other boys did, too. She guessed it was because they were sixteen now, mostly—seventeen, some of them. They were simply growing up.

The bell rang for assembly. In the big auditorium Julie found herself sitting next to Shirley Graham. The hastily assembled orchestra played lustily if unevenly, and the students were all squirming in their places, catching up on vacation news, saying hello to friends. Mr. Stewart, when he finally quieted the disorder, spoke briskly, trying, as he did each year, to disregard the lazy warmth of September and start school off with zest.

Julie listened and looked about with bright eyes, soothed and at ease. She was conscious of being a part of it all, of being a junior, of being a staff member on *Blade*, and of the Academy, always there as a goal beyond it all. Once she leaned toward Shirley and whispered, "It's kind of fun—isn't it—to be back?"

A month later, when an early frost had already painted the maple leaves, it was still fun. Julie was busier than she had ever been before at school. There was hockey practice three times a week, the monthly issue of the school paper to help to prepare, decorations for the Junior Jamboree to devise. Sue Downs, this time, was chairman of the committee. She depended on Julie's ingenuity and said so.

When Julie wailed, "I just haven't got *time*!" Sue passed off the remark with a wave of her small, plump hand. "Nobody has time for anything, but you've just got to help me anyway. I'm so *dumb*."

Julie was flattered—flattered and pleased. She no longer felt as though she were edging into the group around the lunchroom table. She heard her name spoken as often as she heard Connie's or Anne's. It gave her a warm, comfortable, wanted feeling which could even have been a little bit heady if she had allowed herself to be carried away. But she kept her feet firmly planted on the solid ground that Connie had shown her. She tried to be natural and friendly and ready to listen. She'd left off mimicking Marcia or Anne. She wanted, now, to learn to be fully herself.

Only one thing saddened her days—her afternoon homecomings. Try as she would to forget, she still felt emptiness gnaw at her stomach as she left the bus to walk down Deepdale's long lane. Sonny haunted the path, yet he was not there. His bark of greeting was in her ears, the flash of his gold-and-white coat in her eyes. The farm wasn't the same without him.

Even at the bend where the lane swept down into the valley, at the spot where she always paused and let the peace of the place seep through her, she couldn't recapture the old sense of security. Hidden, invulnerable, it had always looked to her before. Now it seemed vacant.

It's the fall, Julie tried to convince herself. It's the dying of the year. It's a sad sort of time. But Julie could remember the fall of a year ago, when the briskness of the air was a challenge, when she wanted to race and run and fling her arms wide because school was finished for another day and she was home with Sonny again.

One afternoon, as she swung down from the bus and automatically poked her hand into the dark interior of the R.D. box, she found a letter addressed, in Mr. Lonsdale's distinctive handwriting, to Tom. The envelope was stiffish, as though it contained an enclosure, and Julie held it against the light and tried to see through it as she hurried down the lane to take it to her dad.

Tom was in the barn, hammering deafeningly, his mouth full of nails. He was repairing a stall.

Julie had to come up close to make him hear her.

"Dad!"

Tom looked up. "Uh?"

"Here's a letter from Mr. Lonsdale. It might be about Sonny. Could you read it now?"

Quite readily, Tom spat out the nails and walked out to the light. He ran his forefinger under the flap of the envelope, ripping it open, while Julie danced with impatience. "He might have won a prize or something," she said.

As her father took out the folded sheet of stationery two oblongs of green cardboard fluttered to the ground. Julie stooped to pick them up, knowing at once what they were.

"Dog-show tickets!" she cried.

Tom was reading silently, engrossed. Julie continued to fidget. "What does he say, Dad?"

"Wait a minute. You can read it for yourself."

"But is Sonny all right?"

"Huh? Sonny? Sure. Sure, he's all right."

"What does he *say* about him?"

Tom handed Julie the letter. "Here. Wants us to come in to the Philadelphia show and see him. Sure nice of him to send us tickets."

It was Julie's turn to be absorbed. She read the letter slowly, then went back and reread one paragraph.

"Sonny is fine. He seems a little listless, but that may well be because he resents his transplantation from the farm to a kennel. You did such a thorough job of training that he responds like a seasoned show dog to Kinney's commands . . ."

"Who's Kinney, Dad?"

"Lonsdale's handler."

"Oh." Julie read on. ". . . though I'm personally a little disappointed in his spirit."

"Spirit? There's nothing wrong with Sonny's spirit! What does he mean?" Julie sounded incensed.

Tom was busy tucking nails between his teeth again. "Just what he says, probably," he mumbled. "It's not easy to uproot a farm-raised dog. It'll take a while."

Julie was reading on. "They've shown him already! Twice!"

136

Tom nodded. "Smaller shows. Philly will be his proving ground." He started to turn away, but Julie stopped him.

"Dad, can we go?"

" 'Course. Why not?" Tom managed to grin in spite of the nails. "Wouldn't miss it for a million bucks," he said.

Slowly Julie walked out of the barn. She went down the path to the yard gate and dropped her books on the grass. Then, suddenly she began to run, down across the still-green meadow to the brook. The air felt cool on her face and her hair blew back so that her ears were cold. It gave her a sense of freedom, of excitement. There was a swift winging up of something inside her heart that was like the flight of a bird.

She would see Sonny again! She hadn't realized that it would mean this much, so deliberately had she been trying to stifle all thought of him. She would see Sonny again! Sonny, walking proud and noble— as Scarlet must have walked—around a dog-show ring. Sonny, with that extra beauty and strength that were his alone, fulfilling his destiny. Sonny flashing his ears for the judges. She could shut her eyes and see him, head high, eyes alert, full of warmth and intelligence.

Joyfully she spread her arms. "Oh Sonny, Sonny!" What had Mr. Lonsdale meant—"disappointed in his spirit"? He couldn't have got really to know Sonny. He must be crazy! She frowned, then remembered the wing chair and felt ashamed. She started along the bank of the stream, kicking at the first bright fallen leaves, awhirl with conflicting thoughts. But deep in her consciousness, beneath the turmoil, was the clear, sweet knowledge—I'll see Sonny again.

The brook wandered through the meadow, and a plank bridge crossed it where the Webster land marched with the Fergusons'. At the bridge Julie paused. In the distance she could see Dick bringing in the cows, and because she had a sudden urge to share her wonderful expectancy with someone, she made a megaphone of her hands and shouted his name.

Dick stopped, turned and waved, then started walking toward her. But Julie couldn't wait. She raced to meet him, calling the news as she ran. "Guess what! We're going to see Sonny shown. In Philadelphia."

Dog shows weren't part of Dick's world. He had to have it explained to him, like a play-by-play description of a football game. When he understood he sympathized with Julie's delight.

"That's great! When is it?"

"The show? Saturday the twenty-first. Two weeks and—" Julie started counting on her fingers—"four days."

Dick's face suddenly changed expression. "But that's the day of the Junior Jamboree," he reminded her.

Julie snapped her fingers. "Oh, heck! The decorations. Well, I'll have to do my share of the work Friday night, that's all." She shrugged it off.

"You'll be back in time for the dance, though? The show won't last into the evening?" If Julie had been less excited, she might have noticed the urgency in Dick's voice.

"I don't know. Might. What does it matter, anyway? I don't care if I miss the dance."

"Oh."

Julie looked at Dick curiously, struck now by the flatness of the monosyllable. "Why?"

Dick was looking down, not directly at her. He was frowning.

"Now don't tell me I haven't got any school spirit! You must know how important to me this dog show is." Julie said it with a laugh, teasing the boy, but she felt vaguely confused.

Dick picked up a stone, kicked up by his toe, and flung it viciously in the direction of the brook. "Oh, sure," he said, still flatly, "I understand."

Julie's eyebrows crinkled, some of her pleasure in sharing the news destroyed. "Then what in the dickens is the matter?"

Dick looked up, full of injured dignity. He almost shouted at her when he said, "I was just thinking you might go to the dance with me, that's all."

His angry tone was so unexpected that it was several seconds before the outburst struck Julie funny. Then her open mouth widened into a laugh, and the impulse to keep on laughing became uncontrollable. "I'm sorry," she gasped, swept into new gales by Dick's continued seriousness. "I really am sorry! But it's the funniest way I ever heard of to ask a girl for a date."

Red crept up Dick's neck until it reached his face and his eyes turned expressionless. Instantly Julie knew that she had offended him. She'd reacted the same way so often herself.

Impulsively she took a step forward, putting a hand on his arm. She was as solemn as he now, her amusement completely quenched. "I *am* sorry, Dick. I wouldn't hurt your feelings for the world."

Dick shook her off. "You didn't—"

But Julie, with a sixth sense that she didn't know she owned, rushed on. It was now or never, and she knew it. "I'd love to go with you, Dick. Honestly I would. I don't see why we couldn't be back in time."

Her brown eyes met the boy's and held them, warm and full of friendliness. She wouldn't—she couldn't!—let the growing shyness within her show in her face.

With a grin Dick relaxed, but he was still embarrassed.

"Okay, swell. We'll talk about it later, huh? I've got to get those cows in now."

He turned and hurried away, while Julie stood watching him for a moment. Then she, too, turned, and, humming a tuneless song under her breath, walked quickly home.

As she lay, that night, curled up in a tense ball under the bedcovers, Julie's mind kept racing along so fast that it was beyond her control. She was quivering with anticipation like a plucked bowstring, and for the life of her she couldn't have told whether the thought of seeing Sonny or of going to the Jamboree with Dick excited her most.

It was Sonny, of course, that made her lie like this, tight and trembling, but then her mind would glance off to things at school, to what the girls would think when she told them—to what they would say. She wouldn't tell them for a while. She'd keep it to herself—her secret—and she'd tell them casually one day at lunch, just before the wonderful evening of the dance.

"I've got a date with Dick."

But it didn't sound casual in her head. It sang. She'd have to be careful of that.

About Sonny and the dog show she'd have to tell them at once. She couldn't keep both things to herself. They'd be mildly interested, but they'd feel none of her excitement. Why should they?

Able to stand the pounding of her heart no longer, she slipped over to the open window, crouched on the sill on her knees, and leaned far out. Moonlight silvered the fields that sloped down to the brook, and the lap of water reached Julie faintly. She put her cheek against the window recess and listened to the sweet sound of it, and to the deep throating of a frog who refused to admit that summer was gone. Beyond the brook the pines clustered, sentries in silhouette, guarding Deepdale, guarding her. Julie breathed deeply, and a sense of peace and strength flowed through her. She felt as much alone as she had ever felt in her life, but not fearfully alone—exultantly. Because when she needed them she had people she could call on—her father, Connie, Dick.

That Dick liked her enough to ask her—that was wonderful, wonderful! That she should be going to the dog show—that at school she was beginning really to fit in—

The multitude of her blessings swept her anew and she prayed a small prayer, out loud: "Oh, God, make me good enough!" Then, suddenly conscious that the soles of her feet were cold, she crept back to bed; the tenseness had gone out of her, and she could close her eyes and go to sleep.

The wonder of having a thrilling private life lasted, for Julie, well through the next two weeks. She wondered if the other girls had such lives, secret, unsuspected, important, and she tried to read the answer in their faces, but it couldn't be done. In the cracked mirror in the girls' washroom her own face looked the same, happier maybe, but not betraying. She marveled at it all.

Beg them as she would to hurry, the days seemed sluggish to Julie. She was glad her extracurricular activities kept her busy in the afternoons. The evenings she filled with homework, with artwork for *Blade*, or with helping Tom to rub down and oil the table he had been making in his cellar workshop. It was to go beside Mr. Lonsdale's wing chair, and he was boyishly proud of his job.

The night he brought it upstairs he stood off and eyed it. "You really like it, Julie? You don't think it looks—well, homemade?"

"Not a bit! I think it's beautiful. I never dreamed you could do anything like that!"

Tom grinned with pleasure at the praise. "I haven't for a long time. Not since I was a kid not much more than Dick's age. I had a girl then—Lolly Randolph, her name was—and I remember I made her a footstool; I don't know why."

Julie looked at him curiously. It had never occurred to her that her dad might have had any girl but her mother. It was odd to grow up and see a parent as a person. Tom began to look younger in her eyes.

He looked especially young on the morning of the Philadelphia Dog Show, when he was scrubbed and shaved and dressed for town. His brown tweed suit was worn at the elbows and the pants were baggy in the back, but the coat fitted his broad shoulders easily, and there was a clean, masculine look about the way his tanned neck rose from the collar of his shirt.

Julie grinned up at him as he helped her into the car. "You look pretty handsome, Dad!" She didn't know why she had said it. She couldn't have said it, with that arch lift of her eyebrows, before Dick had asked her to the dance. But she could see her dad was pleased.

He slammed the car door with a flourish. "You look pretty sweet yourself, baby."

Julie giggled. "Baby!" He hadn't called her that in years.

Tom, pulling in second up to the ridge, replied, "Well, you are just a baby, in spite of the fact you try to act so grown-up." He looked at her out of the corner of his eye as he negotiated the right-angle turn. "What are you so happy about these days, young 'un? Going to the dance with Dick?"

Julie tried not to blush. She shrugged ever so slightly and couldn't keep from smiling. "Seeing Sonny, of course!"

Tom laughed. "I guess it's a bit of both."

And Julie, suddenly serious, agreed. "I guess it is."

They drove into town, extravagantly happy, along the West River Drive beside the loitering Schuylkill. The bright, fragile leaves drifted down and the river looked sleepy and old. Julie felt full to bursting.

The dog show was at Convention Hall, an enormous building out near the university. Cars were wedged closely together in a huge parking lot, which Julie found overpowering.

"Goodness, what a lot of people!"

There were a great many station wagons with dog boxes in the back. There were a great many dogs being walked on leash by their owners. There were a great many owners and a great many visitors like themselves.

Julie clung to Tom's arm as he led her toward the entrance doors. She was glad he was so tall and strong looking and sure of himself. She felt unexpectedly proud.

The vast basement of the hall was hazy and full of confusion. Tom presented their tickets and bought a program, steering Julie expertly through the throng. "I don't see how we'll ever find Sonny in this crowd!" she gasped.

The din of the place was deafening. Dogs were yipping, handlers and owners gossiping in voices pitched above the noise. Judges were bustling about importantly, colored ribbons in their hands.

Tom, pushing Julie forward gently, shouted something in her ear, and Julie shouted back, "I can't hear you!" Tom shook his head. But somehow, with a dogman's sixth sense, he seemed to have found the section where the collies were housed. Julie's heart gave a leap as she caught sight of a graceful plumed tail waving from a stall.

She rushed forward, but the dog turned, and she saw at once that it wasn't Sonny. Just then Tom called to her. "Here are the Lonsdale Kennel boxes," he said.

Julie's eyes swept them quickly. All but two were empty, and she didn't recognize the tri-color collies these contained.

"He must be in the ring already," Tom told her, and started to push his way back into the crowd.

This confusion, this smothering smoke haze, this noise! Julie's heart dropped to the pit of her stomach. Sonny would hate this! She knew it. She wanted to tell her dad. But Tom was well ahead of her, peering over the heads of the people in the aisle to locate the collie ring. On the right a class of bull terriers was being shown, but Julie gave them only a fleeting glance. She could barely glimpse the jaunty stub tail of a cocker spaniel through an opening in the chairs that lined another roped-off square. Tom was waiting for her to catch up. He took her arm and almost pulled her along.

"I've never been to such a *big* show!" she panted.

"Come on," Tom urged. "Hurry up. I don't want to miss Sonny."

Neither did Julie. She edged along by his side eagerly, watching her father flip through the program and then fold the pages back at the place where the listing of collie classes began.

"Here we are," he said finally, but not before Julie had also glimpsed the head of a collie being paraded before a judge.

Julie found Sonny at once. He was one of six dogs in the ring, and on the end of his lead was a pinched kernel of a man with small blue eyes, looking so much like a magazine picture of a jockey that he made Julie's mouth quirk in a smile.

"That must be Kinney," she whispered.

Tom nodded. "Yeh."

Then Julie's eyes were all for the dog. He's one in a million, she thought. One in six million! She wanted to go out and gather him into her arms. She wanted to cry, "Sonny!" and see him break away from Kinney's lead and come racing to her in impetuous bounds. She stood very still at Tom's side.

Tom glanced at the number on Kinney's arm and then at the program. "Let's see how they've got him listed." He paused. Then he pointed out the place to Julie. "Lonsdale's Scarletson." He considered the name. "Makes him sound like a show dog sure."

"He is a show dog. He's going to be a champion. He's beautiful!"

The dogs were moving around the ring now, walking. Julie's eyes shone as she followed Sonny, but she had to look at the other dogs, too, to make sure he was outstanding.

Suddenly she jerked her father's sleeve. "Who's that dog?"

"Which?"

"Number seventy-three."

Tom inspected his program. "Cocoa Colonel of Sweetbriar—" He whistled softly. "Say! D'you know who's being shown against your dog? His own blood brother!"

Julie nodded, her hands clasped. "I was almost sure. Cocoa always had a way of walking—but, Dad, hasn't he grown!"

Tom laughed. "Sonny's grown some, too. It's been a year since you've seen Cocoa—remember?"

"Would they bring him all the way down here from Connecticut?" Julie was impressed.

"They'd take him farther than that if they'd a mind to, I guess. Show dogs do some traveling."

Julie's eyes returned to Sonny as they talked, and then flicked back to Cocoa. There was no doubt that they were almost equally handsome, groomed to the nines as they were, their ruffs brushed out and shining. She glanced at her father and he was frowning slightly. She sensed that he, too, felt it would be a close race. Her heart turned over.

Mr. Lonsdale, in a gray checkered sport coat, appeared behind Tom. Tom turned at his greeting and jerked his head toward the ring. "What's this?" he growled. "Showin' litter mates in the same ring." The grin that finished the sentence belied his tone.

144

Lonsdale shrugged. "It's none of my doing. The Sweetbriar people just know they bought a fine dog. We'll see now," he added, joking, "if you can really pick 'em, Tom."

"If *I* can pick 'em? You chose Sonny yourself out of the three."

Mr. Lonsdale raised his eyebrows, glancing at Julie. "You mean you wouldn't say influence was brought to bear?"

Julie could keep quiet no longer. "Sonny's the best dog! I *know* he is."

The breeder's voice became serious, cool, detached. "I certainly hope so," he admitted.

Julie's insides felt jumbled, like pieces of a jigsaw puzzle tossed together in a box. She edged forward to get a better look at Sonny, but Tom held her back.

"Don't let him see you. You'd throw him off his form."

Mr. Lonsdale had turned to talk to an acquaintance, so Julie brought her mouth up close to her dad's ear. "I know Sonny's best!" she said again, passionately. But Tom didn't reply. His face was stern and unrevealing as he squeezed her arm.

The attention of both of them now concentrated entirely on the ring. Julie discounted the other collies, but it was impossible not to see that Cocoa and Sonny were almost evenly matched. The word had got around the ring that they were litter brothers, and the gallery was straining forward, interested, as the judge singled out the two dogs for minute comparison.

"This is important," Tom told Julie. "They're judging for best of breed."

"So early?" Julie was surprised.

Tom nodded, glancing at his watch. "We were late."

As Kinney walked Sonny back and forth, back and forth, Julie watched the collie closely. Was she imagining it—had Mr. Lonsdale and her dad put the idea into her head—or did Sonny's eyes really lack something of their old sparkle; was there a hint of weariness that never had been there in his days at the farm?

Her hands were clenched, thumbs tucked in. The palms were cold and damp. Cocoa was walking now, the devil-may-care, rollicking quality he'd had as a puppy trained down to a quiet gaiety that made him show to advantage. Julie's brows drew together and her eyes became worried. He wasn't better than Sonny; his carriage wasn't as good nor was his coat as heavy. But he almost *looked* better. It was because he had more zest.

She felt like a traitor, admitting it, even to herself. More zest than Sonny? Never! Yet it was true.

Julie began to watch Kinney with the dog. He was gentle and able. It couldn't be the handler. Or could it? She was swept by confusion and anxiety as the judge knelt before the two collies, now standing side by side, and ran his hand over their bodies, each in turn.

"Feeling the spring of rib," Tom muttered. "That's where Sonny's farm life'll show up."

Julie relaxed a little, but when it came time for the handlers to make the dogs "show"—flash their ears and freeze at attention—she grew concerned again. Cocoa's response was so quick, so animated, that Sonny's seemed slow by comparison.

The judge was writing on his chart, now, busily. He turned finally and walked back to the table. For Julie the suspense became almost unendurable. She found herself clutching Tom's arm, but he apparently hadn't noticed. His eyes were following the judge, too.

There was a purple-and-gold rosette on the table, along with a small silver cup. The judge took them up and walked back across the ring, while the two handlers waited, and Julie closed her eyes.

When she opened them everyone around the ring was clapping, and Kinney had the cup and the rosette in his hand. Unbelievably in his hand! Julie let out her breath in an audible sigh of relief.

"Oh, Dad, I was so afraid!" she breathed.

Tom looked down at her, his face alight with pleasure. "Sonny's superior bone structure finally won out," he told her, "but I'll admit I was worried, too. What's the matter with Sonny, anyway? He's just going through the motions—not really trying at all."

Mr. Lonsdale was coming toward them again, looking more concerned than pleased. "This qualifies Sonny for the working group," he explained. "By rights he should be in line to win there, too, but he isn't showing to advantage. He isn't showing to advantage at all."

Then he turned to Julie. "Want to go back to the box and see him?"

Julie's eyes began to shine. "Oh, please!"

The men, walking ahead, made a path for her, and she almost

skipped up their heels with impatience. Then they turned out from the crowds around the show rings, and into a long line of boxes. Peering around her dad, Julie could see Kinney and Sonny, far at the other end. Suddenly she could wait no longer.

"Sonny!" she cried.

Her young voice rang out, clear as a bell above the hubbub, just as Kinney was whistling his unleased charge into his box. Both Tom and the breeder saw the dog's ears flash up, saw him turn, electrified. A whine in his throat shook itself forth. His nostrils dilated as Julie's scent struck him. Like a whirlwind he came down the alley, a tawny-and-white blaze of speed. Deliriously he flung himself on Julie—barking, writhing, panting. She stumbled back from the force with which he hurled himself against her. He was a vibrant mass of ecstasy, trying to lick her face, moaning and sobbing with joy.

"Sonny."

Julie spoke to the collie in delight, and crouched down on the cement floor to take him in her arms, capturing the whirling paws. But Sonny couldn't be still yet. Tearing away he whizzed round and round her in a bewildering spinning flight, stomach to ground, tongue clamorous with a thousand things he wanted to make Julie understand.

The men stood by and watched, silently, until the collie's hysterical bliss was spent. Julie talked to him in low, soothing tones, stroking his head with both hands.

"Why, Sonny! Sonny boy! You do love me, don't you? You do."

She might have been alone with the dog in the vast hall. She might have had no audience standing over her. She was completely unconscious of the look that passed between Mr. Lonsdale and the handler, but she heard the breeder's words when he spoke to her dad.

"I left him with you too long."

"With Julie—too long," Tom Ferguson corrected him gently. Then they all stood quiet again, looking down.

"That's why he lacked spirit in the ring," Mr. Lonsdale said finally, with no bitterness, but with a voice that was drained of the hope and confidence that Julie felt should have been there. "Isn't it so, Kinney?"

The handler nodded. "Sometimes you find 'em like that."

Mr. Lonsdale walked over to the collie and raised his head in one hand. "You're the finest dog I've ever bred, boy," he said very slowly, "but I'm afraid you'll never prove it. I'd have liked to make a champion of you. I would that, boy." He squeezed the long muzzle gently and dropped his hand. Then, smiling sadly, he turned to his handler. "Think we'd better call it a day?"

Before Kinney could reply Julie was on her feet, her eyes burning. "He *is* a champion!" she insisted. "He's everything a collie should be. He deserves to win!" She turned from Mr. Lonsdale to Kinney. "Maybe this afternoon he'll be better. I'm sure he will. Now that he's seen me."

But Kinney shook his head. "Less chance now than before. But even before we was licked, Miss. I've seen 'em like that. All fire and flame for one person. For the rest, nothing."

Julie felt tears sting her eyelids. She blinked them back hard. She tried to concentrate on what Kinney was going on to say.

"At Baltimore and Boston it was the same. He won, yes, but the competition wasn't keen. He'll obey my commands because he's trained, but he acts like he's bored. He *is* bored. You, that's what he's got his mind on." He pointed a finger at Julie, waving it. "You, all the time."

Julie could feel the warmth of Sonny's body pressed against her thigh. Her hand, on his ruff, sought for the soft, close hair under the harsh outer coat. The words that came from her lips weren't hers at all. They came from something hidden inside her that forced itself out.

"Let me handle him this afternoon," she heard herself begging Mr. Lonsdale. "He'll show for me. I know he will! I'm sure he can win!"

All three men stared at Julie. Tom Ferguson looked plainly astonished, Kinney looked thoughtful, and Mr. Lonsdale seemed half amused, half intrigued. Finally the breeder chuckled and said: "What do you think Kinney? It might work."

Then suddenly, everybody was talking at once.

"Don't be ridiculous. She's too young." It was Tom's deep voice, booming out.

"She's young, yes. But the dog will show for her. I'd stake my reputation on that." Kinney spoke slowly, still looking at Julie, who squirmed under the searching gaze of his blue eyes. The old, creeping timidity was ready to replace her momentary flash of confidence. Her fingers tightened convulsively in Sonny's ruff, but she couldn't speak, couldn't take back her offer now.

"I'd like to try, Dad," she said, keeping her voice as level as possible. "Sonny deserves his chance."

Mr. Lonsdale also turned toward the farmer. "It's up to you, Tom."

"Dad, please!"

"You've never been in a ring. You don't know a thing about showing."

"I've been to shows."

"They were different." Tom was frowning, now, darkly. "Smaller."

"Mr. Kinney could teach me, maybe."

"How much time," asked Philip Lonsdale, "have we got?"

Tom pulled out his watch and with that gesture he agreed. "Almost three hours," he said.

It was the busiest three hours Julie had ever spent. Her dad and Mr. Lonsdale left her with Kinney, and the little man led her from ring to ring, pointing out details of handling a dog, explaining the meaning of gestures and orders from the judge. Then he took her back to Sonny, and he pretended to be the judge himself, while she walked the collie, ran him, arranged his forefeet, back legs, and head in a show dog's stance. She whistled, and Sonny flashed his ears, alert and questioning. She commanded him to stand still, and he stood at attention, obedient, understanding. Kinney sighed sorrowfully, and Julie looked at him, frightened for an instant, but he only muttered, "That's beautiful, Miss. He never worked for me like that."

There was no time for a proper lunch. Tom came back with sandwiches and pint cartons of milk and the three of them ate, leaning against the side of the dog box. Afterward Julie could never remember what the sandwiches were made of.

The sketchy meal finished, Kinney returned to his coaching. "There's not much to it, really," he tried to comfort his pupil when he could feel her getting nervous. "Just follow the leader if you get confused. And if you can't hear the judge make him repeat. It won't hurt Sonny's chances if *you* aren't letter-perfect. Just so he is."

Half an hour before the working group was to be called, Mr. Lonsdale walked back to the collie's box again. He looked relaxed and unconcerned, and he grinned broadly when he came close enough to sense the tension shared by the two men and the girl.

"Take it easy, child," he told Julie. "This isn't a matter of life and death. We're taking a sporting chance, that's all." He patted her shoulder affectionately.

But Julie's eyes were large and serious. She was still dumbfounded at her own boldness, but she was determined to conquer her fear for Sonny's sake. She stood and listened to the conversation of the men in an anxious daze. How could they sound so controlled, so unperturbed? She'd never understand adults—not even, she believed, when she was really grown-up herself.

Mr. Lonsdale led her father away after a while, and with his retreating back Julie's last thread tying her to security snapped. Kinney was a stranger, kind and consoling, but he was a stranger after all.

A bag of lead was tied to her ribs, weighing her down with fear. The numbered armband which Kinney pinned on her was an alien thing, terrifying in itself.

"Eighty-seven," she croaked through dry lips. "D'you think that's lucky?"

"Seven's lucky," Kinney told her, cheerfully. "Seven-come-eleven." But Julie didn't hear him. She was trying to still her trembling, to govern the weakness of her knees.

Somehow, when Sonny's leash was in her hand, she felt better. It was something to hang on to, that lead, something familiar to grasp.

At the entrance to the ring everything seemed to be in confusion. Of the twenty-five possible entries in the working-dog group Julie was sure that at least a dozen were in a hopeless tangle. She saw an Eskimo, a German shepherd, a magnificent and disdainful Great Dane, and a cumbersome Saint Bernard in the chaos. It seemed odd that they should all be pitted against Sonny. She would have felt more at home had she been showing him in an all-collie class.

Kinney stayed by her side as long as possible, whispering encouragement into her ear. Somehow she found herself within the ring itself, and gradually the tangle dissolved, and a thin man handling a Briard took his place by her side.

Julie felt, for a moment when she caught his glance, absurdly young. But then she saw his eyes sweep over Sonny, and she was conscious of a flash of pleasure because of his obvious admiration for the dog.

The judge was working with a pencil, making notations on his chart. Julie watched him closely, but she scarcely saw him nod his head. It seemed to her that by common consent the handlers started walking their dogs in a circle. Sonny seemed to fall in line automatically, and Julie found herself walking, too.

She concentrated her attention on the dog, trying to make herself small, insignificant, so that he would show to advantage. He was carrying his tail well down, with no swirl, as was proper. The movement of his body was sound; he walked with a jaunty step, looking up at her happily.

"Good boy!" she whispered to him, and with the words a spring that had wound her tight as a top was suddenly released. She could breathe again; she could forget herself, forget the gallery of onlookers, because she wanted so desperately to be worthy of the confidence in Sonny's eyes.

"Keep the dog between yourself and the judge, whatever you do."

She remembered Kinney's instructions and obeyed them, alert to any new order from the man with the pad. She knew, when his eyes rested on Sonny, that he was watching the angle of the collie's hocks. How many times her dad had told her, "They should move like pistons." She thought that surely they were moving like pistons now.

The handlers lined up with their dogs in front of the judge, and the blur of faces beyond the ropes began to separate into individuals for Julie. She could see people looking at Sonny, looking at the Great Dane, at the German shepherd. She couldn't see her dad or Mr. Lonsdale, but she caught Kinney's eye and he nodded and grinned, clasping his hands in front of his chest in a gesture of approval. She was grateful to him and she sighed in relief. She must be doing all right.

The judge was going over each dog individually, feeling the spring of rib, judging the bone structure. Sonny stood like a veteran, quiet and poised. When the judge had passed on the dog looked up at her, a question in his eyes, and she nodded.

"Good boy!" she said again.

With the other handlers, then, Julie took her turn in running Sonny down the ring and walking him back. The judge watched each dog separately, following it with sharp, shrewd eyes, making more notes on his chart.

Julie's heart began to pound again. She wished she could read the man's mind. She had no idea how Sonny might stack up among all these different breeds. She had no basis for comparison. She knew that for her he was unequaled, but that might not mean a thing.

The judge glanced at his chart again, while the handlers fidgeted, arranging their dogs to advantage, soothing them, scolding them, fussing over them. Julie stood perfectly still, big-eyed, waiting, and Sonny stood quiet beside her, looking up into the girl's face, ever so gently waving his tail.

The judge looked up and beckoned to the handler of the Eskimo, a tall, gaunt woman with an enormous mole on her left cheek. She jerked her head and stepped forward, followed by her dog. The man handling the Dane also walked toward the judge. Then Julie jumped as a voice rapped out a number. "Eighty-seven, please."

She joined the other two, and again the selected dogs were put through their paces. The routine, once understood, now seemed simple to Julie, and Sonny reacted brilliantly to every command. When the collie flashed his ears and froze at attention, she heard a murmured "Ah" from the gallery. She didn't blame the onlookers. She could have cheered for him herself.

Only the judge's face was expressionless as he reconsidered each dog. The Dane, Julie could sense without understanding, was an exceptionally fine specimen. He had a thoroughbred's arrogance, and the muscles under his glossy coat moved like silk rippling. The Eskimo was an unknown quantity to her. He seemed foreign, unlike a pet, almost wild. But the judge was running his hands over the compact body carefully. He must be good.

Again the girl stood quiet, waiting. Her nervousness, intense before she had entered the ring, had diminished until she felt nothing, no self-consciousness, even no fear of the outcome of the showing. The collie's nearness was like a spreading warmth, surrounding her. She hadn't had time to relish it before, but now she recognized the reason for the deep happiness that crept through her. They were together again.

Julie scarcely noticed that the judge had risen and was walking back toward the table at the side of the ring. The man had dropped his chart and picked up a shining silver bowl which was the winner's trophy before she realized that he was coming toward them, toward Sonny and her, with the prize in his hands.

The gallery clapped vigorously as she accepted it, and she stammered, "Th-thank you!" in pleasure, but not in especial surprise. She had none of the weak-kneed feeling of disbelief that had hit her upon winning the poster contest. Sonny was worthy, magnificent. This was his due.

The silver felt cool and heavy against her arm. She tightened Sonny's lead and started for the ring entrance, searching anxiously now for her dad and Mr. Lonsdale. She found them, with Kinney, close to the ropes, waiting to receive her as she came out with the dog.

Julie smiled at them, tremulous now that it was over. She handed the trophy to Mr. Lonsdale at once, but she kept Sonny's leash in her hand as the four of them walked back to the collie's box. All the men were praising her, after their fashion. Tom pinched her cheek and said, "I'm proud of you, baby." Kinney said: "There! Didn't I say you could do it, Miss!" and Mr. Lonsdale teased her: "A cool customer, a very cool customer. You might think, Julie, that you got a silver cup every day in the week."

Julie looked up at him, serious. "It's Sonny's, not mine. I knew he could do it. I *knew* he could."

Kinney nodded. "With you beside him. Not with me, Miss. And not alone."

Mr. Lonsdale looked at the handler sharply. "You're sure of that, Kinney?"

"Sure as I can be, sir. Haven't I spent two months with that dog!"

Julie's eyes darkened, became almost resentful. She started to speak, to defend the collie, but something in the breeder's face stopped her. Mr. Lonsdale was looking from Kinney to her dad.

"There's only one answer to that, Tom," he said very slowly and evenly. "The girl and the dog belong together, just as we've known all along."

Julie looked down blindly. His words couldn't mean—they *couldn't* mean—

But she could see Sonny, head high and tail flying, cantering over the hills at Deepdale, climbing the ridge in joyous bounds. She could hear the screech of the school-bus brakes and see the collie run to meet her. She could feel his wet tongue as he caressed her, know again the wild freedom of racing with him down the hill, pebbles tumbling in their wake as they pulled up at the bridge, breathless. Hope burned in her heart, delirious, uncontrollable, until, as she raised her head, she saw again the trophy which Mr. Lonsdale still held in his hand.

"Sonny's a show dog...bred to a great tradition...one collie in a thousand." Isolated phrases of her father's pumped into Julie's head. "A certain champion...his heritage." The girl's hands were clasped together so tight that they hurt as she tried to say in words what she felt.

"It wouldn't be fair," she insisted, "to take him back. It wouldn't be fair to Sonny, to keep him forever on the farm." She repeated what her dad had said about his heritage. "He ought to be famous," she said. "He can be. He will be."

But the breeder shook his head. "Back in the kennel, he'd only eat his heart out again. Kinney's right, Julie. He's yours." Then his eyes began to twinkle. "He's yours, that is, conditionally. I'm a good enough businessman to attach a string. He's yours if your dad will let you show him for me, say once or twice a year, and if he'll manage him for me as a Lonsdale Kennel stud." He looked back to Ferguson. "How about it, Tom?"

Tom grinned. "What can I say? What would I want to say? Of course."

Julie rode home with her arm around Sonny.

Tom insisted on celebrating by stopping at an inn for dinner, so it was dark when they reached the farm. On the stoop, as they came down the ridge, Julie could see Dick waiting. The headlights picked out his figure, and Tom chuckled. "He's been on the hot seat, sure."

Dick was obviously nervous when the car pulled up at the yard gate, but shouted, "Gosh, I thought you were drowned!" Then he saw Sonny and annoyance fled his face. "Well, would you look who's here!"

"He's back to stay!" Julie cried as she scrambled out of the car. Then she left her dad to the further explanations as she dashed into the house to change her clothes.

She flung the garments she took off anywhere—her jacket, her sweater, her skirt. She ripped off her brown knee socks and pulled on pantyhose with fingers that trembled in spite of the need to be careful. Then she slipped into her sandals and ran into the bathroom for a hasty scrubbing. Finally she stepped into her party dress.

It was the same dress—the plaid cotton—the only long dress Julie had. It was going on two years old now—and Julie was going on sixteen. She had to draw in her breath when she fastened it at the waist, and she looked at it critically. Cotton. It was wrong for fall, but it couldn't be helped. It was still becoming, making her hair brighter than usual and her eyes dark.

Dick was pacing up and down the living room when she came downstairs, and her dad was just slamming in from the barn with a package under his arm.

"Before you go," Tom said rapidly, sounding ill at ease, "I've got something for you, Julie. When I—when I had this done, I didn't know we'd be bringing the collie home." He hesitated and thrust out the bulky paper-wrapped parcel.

There was a question in Julie's eyes as they met her father's. She couldn't imagine what the package could be. "A present?" she asked tentatively. "For me?"

Tom nodded, and Julie walked over to the desk with the parcel and put it down on the blotter as she undid the cord. Then she folded back the paper.

"Oh, Dad!"

In matching frames of natural wood were three of Julie's sketches of Sonny.

"I stole 'em," Tom confessed, still sounding embarrassed. "And as I said, I didn't think we'd be coming back with the real article."

"But it was *sweet* of you!" Julie cried, feeling that her words were inadequate. There was a burning, tingling sensation at the tip of her nose, and she was afraid that she might burst into tears.

Dick broke the spell by taking the picture she held from her. "Wow!" he breathed. "Framed up these look professional. Julie, you're really *good*."

"Sure she is," said Tom. Then, abruptly, he changed the subject. "Want me to drive you kids over, Dick?"

"Thanks, but I've got Pop's car," Dick replied grandly. "I got my license last week."

Julie slipped her arms into her old green tweed coat before either of the men could jump to help her. She laid her cheek against her dad's, then, with her skirts ballooning about her, sank down to throw her arms once more around Sonny.

"Hey!" Dick scolded, suddenly masculine. "We've got to get going. Or would you rather stay home with the dog?"

Julie jumped up. "I'm not sure," she laughed, unembarrassed. "I'd like to do both."

Dick looked at her dad in a way that said, "Women!" and grabbed her hand authoritatively. "Come on."

The school, in the wing where the gym was situated, was ablaze with lights. Excitement pervaded the dim, familiar corridors, and from a background of music and laughter voices burst like firecrackers popping. Julie dropped her coat in the locker room with only the most casual inspection of her hair.

She had forgotten her lipstick! She bit at her lips to make them red, then hurried into the crowded gym to find Dick.